THE PROMISE OF VICTORY

Published in Nashville, Tennessee, by Thomas Nelson, Inc., Publishers, and distributed in Canada by Word Communications, Ltd., Richmond, British Columbia, and in the United Kingdom by Word (UK), Ltd., Milton Keynes, England.

Scripture quotations are from the NEW KING JAMES VERSION of the Bible. Copyright © 1979, 1980, 1982, 1990 Thomas Nelson, Inc., Publishers.

Quoted material in Chapter 19 comes from *The Screwtape Letters* by C. S. Lewis (New York: TIME Inc., 1963).

Library of Congress Cataloging-in-Publication Data

Grant, Jean.
    The promise of victory : a novel / Jean Grant.
      p. cm. — (The Salinas Valley saga ; bk. 3)
    ISBN 0-7852-8103-7
    1. World War, 1939-1945—California—San Francisco—
Fiction. 2. Young women—California—San Francisco—
Fiction. 3. San Francisco (Calif.)—Fiction. I. Title.
II. Series: Grant, Jean. Salinas Valley saga ; bk. 3.
PS3557.R2663P77   1995
813'.54—dc20   94-46365
                                                  CIP

Printed in the United States of America
2 3 4 5 6 7 - 01 00 99 98 97 96

THE PROMISE OF VICTORY

JEAN GRANT

THOMAS NELSON PUBLISHERS
Nashville • Atlanta • London • Vancouver

Chapter One

A few families clustered on the platform at the Soledad Railroad Station. It was a hot September afternoon. Summer vacation was over, and parents were seeing their children off to college. But every eye turned at least once to Ellen Hanlon. The smiles of the men were openly admiring; most of the women smiled too, but a few shrugged and glanced away.

Ellen was a pretty girl. Her softly curved figure was well defined by the simple linen sheath she wore. Bouncy gold waves framed her heart-shaped face and set off the ivory complexion she carefully protected with a wide-brimmed straw hat. Her mouth was small; her pert nose tilted up just a trifle; her clear blue eyes always seemed to take in everything around her all at once.

A young man jumped onto the train and reached down to Ellen. She took the familiar hand he offered and stepped lightly into the waiting car. The families seeing them off smiled at the young man too. Ron Stephens' face was as tanned as Ellen's was fair, and his sandy hair was faded to almost the same tawny beige from working all summer in his father's lettuce fields.

The people of Soledad weren't accustomed yet, in the autumn of 1940, to khaki. But Ron wore his crisp new uniform easily, if proudly. His brand-new gold Second Lieutenant's bars gleamed in the sun, dazzling the people who watched.

Ellen turned to wave to her parents, then followed Ron into the passenger car. She studied his face as she slipped into the window seat he offered. As he sat down, he carefully edged well over toward the aisle to avoid crowding her.

As the train rolled away from the station, Ellen picked up a newspaper that had been left behind and began to fan herself. "Won't it be great to get up to San Francisco and out of this heat?" she remarked. *Imagine*, she thought, *talking to Ron about the weather*.

"Might be warm in the city too." His tone was friendly, no more, no less.

"It must be terribly hot in that uniform."

He shrugged. "Have to wear it when I report in at Fort Mason, and I couldn't see trying to change at the depot."

"And besides, you have to show off the bars," she teased.

"I did spend four hard years in ROTC earning them." He forced a smile. "Ellen, I am proud to wear my country's uniform. Why shouldn't I be? It's a great country, and I'm glad to be able to defend it."

"Sometimes I think you'll be disappointed if we don't get involved in this war between Germany and England," she chided. *There it is, already—the old quarrel,* she thought. *Why did this stupid war have to happen anyway? If it weren't for that . . .* No. Ellen was too honest to blame their break-up on the war alone.

"We'll have to fight eventually." Ron wouldn't let go of the subject. "Hitler obviously intends to take over all of Europe."

"So what?" Her wide eyes turned from Ron and his irritating logic. She gazed at the green fields flying past. *At least,* she thought, *all this war talk has improved the economy. Crops are selling for a decent price again, and growers can make a decent living and pay their help a decent wage.* "What difference does it make to us, Ron, which country controls what piece of Europe?" She couldn't bring herself to yield without a response either. "It isn't our war."

They'd been having the same argument for a year now. Ellen could actually date it. It had begun last September, on the train back to Berkeley. Then the knowing smiles of the people of Soledad who sent them off to college had meant something. And Ellen and Ron had sat much closer on that train going north.

They had been high school sweethearts, despite the half-hidden opposition of Ron's mother. Ellen consciously brushed off snatches of ugly gossip overheard when she came into earshot. She refused to listen, willing herself not to be hurt by those unkind words.

Ellen smiled as she recalled how she and Ron had casually avoided each other at church or town socials when his mother was present. She recalled group dates that subtly turned into twosomes. The whole high school seemed to enjoy the informal conspiracy to keep Mrs. Stephens in the dark. *But,* Ellen still wondered, *why does she dislike me so? Why does she repeat that hateful gossip? Does she really know something about my mother, my real mother?*

Then Ron had gone off to study engineering at Cal. She had missed him so much those first two years—too much, her mother told her, for a girl still in high school.

Ron had come home for the summer, and Ellen had been so thrilled that this "college man" still sought her out. She lived for Christmas vacation, semester break, and Easter week when Ron came back to Soledad, and they met at the homes of their friends. Then, in September of 1938, she went to Berkeley with him. They didn't have to meet in secret anymore, and conversations never subtly shifted when Ellen joined chattering groups on campus. Ron had been ignoring his mother's disapproval for years; Carrie Hanlon's warnings to Ellen about their being too young to get serious fell on the deaf ears of a deliriously happy eighteen year old.

Of course they would wait until Ron had his degree, and Ellen had every intention of finishing the nurse's training she was about to start. By then, Ron would have a steady job. Ellen planned to work a few years until they had a nest egg set aside. Then they would get married and start a family when they were "ready." It was such a pretty package, the American dream, all tied up with a red, white, and blue bow.

A year ago we still had the package, she told herself, though even then the ribbons had begun to fray. There were little things, like the day he caught her with a cigarette. "All the girls do it," she told him.

"They do not, and you know it."

"You mean nice girls in Soledad don't. I'm not in Soledad anymore, Ron. Daddy isn't watching me."

Ron frowned as she deliberately puffed smoke in his face. "I hate to see you hurting yourself just to 'proclaim your independence,' as you like to say. And you *are* a nice girl. Why shouldn't you act like one?"

"Am I?" she muttered. "I thought everybody knew my mother was no good. 'Like mother, like daughter.' Isn't that what your mother always told you?"

Ron had always defended Ellen against the whispers and sideways glances. "That's silly gossip," he had told her. "She doesn't know anything about your real mother, and if she did, what difference would it make? You're you, yourself. That's all that matters."

Ellen quit smoking when he was around. In fact, she quit almost entirely. *He's right,* she admitted. *I don't really like it. It is a dirty, expensive habit, and I just do it to prove I can.*

Their disagreement about religion was harder to handle. Her biology classes fascinated her, and she loved sharing all she was learning with Ron. She actually took a perverse delight in getting a rise out of him when she shared her new gospel of evolution.

In Soledad the high school science teacher was considered a "free-thinker" because he had read Darwin. At Cal her professors backed up faith in science with what seemed, to Ellen, to be irrefutable facts. And Ron was so stubborn, so unreasonable.

"But everybody knows, now, that the Bible's just a collection of myths and fables," she had insisted. *Yes, that's when we started to drift apart*, she conceded to herself. *But we could have gotten around that.*

It was true they hadn't argued that much about religion. She had always taken it for granted that when the time came, they'd go back to Soledad and get married in the little Methodist church they'd grown up in. *Mrs. Stephens can like it or lump it*, Ellen concluded. And when they had children they would take them to Sunday school. Just because she realized now that God, if there were a God, could not be kept in a neat Methodist box didn't mean she no longer appreciated the teachings of Jesus. Ron would learn to be tolerant.

A year ago, though, Ellen had already begun to understand that while what Ron believed might not matter to her, her lack of belief did matter to him. *Still, we'd have worked that out, if it just hadn't been for the war.*

That first year at Cal their lives had revolved separately around their classes and together around the co-op. Ron had moved into the student co-op dorm purely to save money. A few years before, at the bottom of the Great Depression, a few Cal students, with some help from the YMCA, had organized and leased an apartment building to provide themselves with low-cost housing. Economic necessity had made the enterprise flourish, and in the winter of 1937 the first women's dorm, Stebbins Hall, had opened.

The co-op concept came naturally to the students from Soledad, whose fathers had been forming farm co-ops for decades. Ron had plunged into student management with a passion. Naturally Ellen had moved into Stebbins, and into the lively social life of the organization.

Oh, that first year! They worked together tending buildings and grounds and preparing meals in the co-op's new central kitchen. They played together at picnics and parties, in spite of Ron's stubborn refusal to please her by learning to dance. When Ellen and Ron went back to Soledad for the summer, most of the little town still smiled knowingly at the faithful twosome.

Hitler had invaded Poland last fall, on the first of September. Ron had been outraged; Ellen had insisted it was not America's problem. Ron's ROTC unit stopped being a means to a cheap education and became what Ellen called an obsession. Ellen joined a student peace group. "War is not the way to solve the world's problems," she insisted. And who could quarrel with that? *Ron could,* she recalled.

She looked at him in the seat next to her, deeply absorbed in a book. *We were such kids then, when I first went to Berkeley. Why, I'd scarcely been farther from home than Salinas. I was so naive.* She frowned ever so slightly. *But I grew up during those two years.*

Ellen had learned so much from those classes taught by some of the most brilliant minds in the country. *Especially from the science classes,* she thought. *What a wonderful world they opened up for me, what a wonderfully complex world. Maybe things were simpler in Soledad, where God spoke and the farmers jumped. But in the real world, the world I found in Berkeley, we individual human beings are what counts.*

Ron had been right about the co-op, though. He had

said you really got to know people by working with them so closely. She remembered Sarah Cohn, Patsy Wong, Maria Gomez, and Kimiko, of course, thrown together in the dorm from backgrounds she had never dreamed existed, full of ideas she had never thought of.

But Ron didn't grow, at least not in the same direction. She glanced at him. She gathered from the picture on the cover of his book that it was about flying, his latest passion. *He still thinks like a farm boy from the Salinas Valley. He's lucky, in some ways, at least. He still believes all that stuff about "God and country."* Now he was on his way to Texas, to learn to fly airplanes for the Army Air Corps, and she was going to study nursing at the University of California Medical Center in San Francisco.

Ron closed his book. "Excited about starting nursing school?" he asked her.

"I guess so. Sometimes I wish I were going back to Berkeley instead. There are so many classes I'd still like to take, so much more I'd like to learn. But then, I'll be learning a lot of biology, and psychology, too, in nursing school. And being in San Francisco will be stimulating. I'll be able to go to the theater and to the symphony—maybe I'll even try to get ushering tickets for the opera."

"Student nurses don't have much time for 'culture,'" he reminded her.

"Nursing school isn't like it used to be, Ron. When my sister, Marianne, was a student, all she did was work on the wards. If all I wanted to do was be a floor nurse, I could have gone to a hospital in San Jose like she did. I'd be almost finished now. But Cal's nursing school is different. I'll have a real education when I get through."

"Sometimes I wonder why you decided on nursing at all, Ellen," he mused. "I know you have always wanted to help people, but you're so hungry for knowledge. Somehow I thought you might have chosen teaching."

"I probably chose nursing because of my sister. I always admired Marianne, going off to China to nurse the heathen and preach the gospel to them. When I was little it sounded so romantic." She shook her head, and the golden waves danced across her forehead. "I even used to picture myself in a Salvation Army bonnet. Can you imagine?"

"As a matter of fact, I can. They do good work, Ellen."

"Oh, I know, Ron, especially the social work. But the gospel's so old-fashioned, and the Chinese would be just as well off without it . . ."

"Would they?" he interrupted. "Do you really believe that?"

I thought we had agreed to disagree about religion. She pretended not to have heard him. "I think the future of medicine is in prevention. Ignorance is really the basic cause of suffering. Public health nursing, education, helping people to live better so they don't get sick—that's what I think I'd like to do."

Ron went back to his book, and Ellen reached for the needlepoint bag she had tucked under the seat. Gran had made it for her, and Ellen studied again the intricate floral design carefully worked in pastel silk. Gran, Anna McLean, wasn't really her grandmother. She was Carrie Hanlon's stepmother, and Carrie was Ellen's adopted mother, not her biological mother.

Ellen knew they all loved her as much as if she were their own blood. *If there were a God who actually paid attention to us down here, I would thank him for my family,* Ellen told herself. *But then, if there were a God like that, why would he have taken my real mother away from me?* She took Hemingway's new novel out of the bag. *And if there were a God, surely he would put a stop to war and the suffering it causes to innocent people.*

For Whom the Bell Tolls was about war. It seemed like everyone was talking about war, and most of them, like Ron, were excited by it. They thought going halfway across the world to kill, and probably to be killed, was somehow heroic and glorious. Sure, there were wicked people in the world, and Herr Hitler did sound like one of them, but . . .

Uncle Tim had been in the last war, Ellen recalled. When he talked about it now he said it had made a man out of him. But Gran's oldest son, Ellen's step-uncle, had gone to France in 1917, too, and had come back a broken man. Gran still spoke of him now and then and of how he had been sick from poison gas and addicted to morphine. Ellen didn't know the details, only that he had disappeared the night Uncle Tim and Aunt Nancy were married; he was never heard from again. *If war didn't kill outright,* she thought, *it often did worse.*

She gazed out the train window. They had left the broad green fields of the Salinas Valley behind, and Ellen heaved an unconscious sigh of relief. She loved her family, but they were so tied to that infernal dirt. And Soledad, that smug little backwater town, revolved around Grange meetings, American Legion dances, and ice cream socials at the Methodist Church!

"Pretty, isn't it?" Ron commented, waving toward the plum trees sagging under their lush purple load. "The Santa Clara Valley wouldn't be a bad place to live, would it? More trees than at home."

"Yes, it's better than Soledad, I guess," Ellen answered. She didn't voice the rest of the thought: *Anything would be.* "But why not San Francisco, or maybe the East Bay? Or why settle down at all yet? With your engineering degree, you could get a job anywhere. When you get this flying thing out of your system you could go all over the world building things."

"Maybe that's why I want to do my part to save that world, Ellen. So I can go out and build things. But that kind of life isn't forever. It's all right for a few years, maybe, but home is forever, and home, for me, is the Salinas Valley."

"It's fine for you and Mom and Dad, I guess, but not for me, Ron. Two years ago, when I first went to Berkeley, it was like stepping into wonderland—the campanile was reaching for the sky, and I wanted to reach up with it. Everywhere I turned there was something new to see, to learn, to absorb. Buildings—beautiful buildings. Sather Gate led not just to a bunch of lecture halls and labs, but to a whole new world. And there were books everywhere, and no one even suggested that some of them weren't 'suitable.' And people, Ron, the people! People from all over the world who showed me that the Salinas Valley isn't the whole world. And it isn't my world, Ron. Not anymore."

"Don't you see the contradiction, Ellen? You want to

be part of the whole world, and the whole human race. You condemn Soledad for its small-town self-absorption. And yet you insist Europe's war isn't our problem."

"But Ron, wars don't really change things. They don't solve problems. I want to be part of a civilized world, not brutality, not chaos."

"I hope and pray," he whispered, "that you get the chance."

Their train skirted the edge of San Francisco Bay. On her right Ellen could see the cranes hovering over the newly busy shipyards at Hunters Point. But Ellen preferred to look to her left, toward the west, where neat workmen's cottages climbed step-wise up the steep hills of the Bay View district. *A good place*, she thought, *for a visiting nurse to teach hygiene and first aid. These are decent people who want to improve themselves.*

Dirty faces with sunken cheeks flashed through her mind. Just a few short summers ago, in the depths of the Great Depression, she had helped her mother ladle out soup on their back porch for the hungry children of migrant farm workers. *Those children always seemed to be sick*, she recalled.

Ellen had helped her sister, Marianne, and her husband who were home on a brief furlough from China. They had spent their few weeks of vacation giving smallpox vaccinations, diphtheria shots, and TB tests. In the evening after the day's lettuce harvest was in, Marianne and Paul had taught the exhausted women how to cook nourishing meals from cheap ingredients and how to prevent infection and contagion. They had preached too.

Ellen could not see that the preaching did much good, but the shots and the classes did help.

Yes, Ellen told herself, *that was when I decided to be a public health nurse, and those were the people I wanted to help. But thanks to the New Deal, times are better now. If we can just keep out of this war we can lick sickness and starvation with technology.*

The train finally pulled into the San Francisco Depot. Ellen put the unread book back into her bag. "Give me your baggage check, and I'll pick up your suitcases and get you into a cab," Ron offered.

"Thanks, but that's not necessary. We shipped the trunk up a few days ago. It should already be at the nurses' dorm. I'll just walk over to Market Street and take a streetcar." She glanced at a note in her hand. "Judah Street. It runs within a couple of blocks of the dorm."

They walked together the few blocks to Market Street. Ellen gazed at the broad thoroughfare—streetcar tracks down the middle, traffic from curb to curb, tall buildings rising on either side. She took a deep breath of air fresh with salt spray and energy.

Ron took her arm. His touch was casual, but protective. She relished the brief touch, gone as soon as they reached the safety of the mid-street platform. He waited with her until the Judah car approached, and then he took her arm once again. She turned to face him. Impulsively she stretched up to kiss him. "You're off to serve your country after all."

He smiled, but she realized his eyes were sad. "Just friends, Ellen?"

"Good friends, Ron. Always."

Then he let his lips touch her forehead and linger for a moment as the streetcar pulled to a stop. "Always," he promised.

Chapter Two

The couple of blocks from the streetcar line to the student nurses' dorm was straight up Third Avenue. The compact medical center was very different from the sprawling Berkeley campus she had come to love, but this place, too, reached for the sky.

Mount Sutro loomed dead ahead. Across the street, the University of California Hospital seemed built right into the face of the rocky cliff. Down along Parnassus Avenue the nearly new clinic building hid from her view the old medical and dental school which had survived the 1906 earthquake. *How?* she wondered. The whole complex looked like it would slide down the steep hill at the slightest tremor.

Ellen found Kimiko Ohata waiting in their room at the back of the square brick building across the street from the hospital. Her roommate was standing by the window. Ellen joined her. "Wow! How did we rate a view like this?" she asked.

Just below them a broad swath of green marked Golden Gate Park. Over the treetops they could see most of San Francisco's Richmond district where bright pastel houses held hands along the streets, like children playing circle games around brilliant flower gardens. Beyond lay another patch of evergreen that was the Presidio. Above the wooded mounds of the Presidio, the south tower of the new Golden Gate Bridge pierced the low clouds that hovered there.

"We'll have to keep the shades down or we'll never get any studying done," Kimiko laughed. "Which bed do you want?"

"The one you don't have clothes scattered all over." Ellen laughed and dropped her bag on the empty bed. She glanced behind the door. "I see my trunk's here. I'd better start unpacking. Tomorrow's registration."

"Yes. I suppose I'll get tired of the view—eventually." Kim stood on tiptoe to hang her crisp new blue uniforms and white aprons on the closet bar. Kim always seemed to be on tiptoe, scarcely five feet tall, incredibly slim, a petite whirling tornado. Her straight black hair and darting black eyes were a startling contrast to Ellen's fairness.

Their backgrounds were no less opposite, though they had grown up less than fifty miles apart. Ellen's father had owned his ever-expanding acreage in the Salinas Valley for forty years. Kimiko's father had been in the United States nearly that long, but the law prohibited his owning even the little building in which he ran his grocery store in King City, down at the south end of the same long valley.

Yet the two girls had been instantly drawn to each

other. Though both came from solidly middle-class families, the expense of a university education, even at a free state school, was a strain on family budgets still recovering from the Great Depression. The new girls' co-op dorm had been a godsend.

"Remember when we moved into Stebbins?" Kim reminisced. "Neither of us knew a soul in the house, but we both liked that room way up on the top floor because we could see the campus from it. Would you have chosen it, though, if you'd known your roommate would be Japanese?"

"You know, I'm honestly not sure," Ellen replied. "Patsy just said you were another pre-nursing student, and were from King City." Ellen smiled again. "I thought we'd have a lot in common."

"The strange thing is that we found out we did."

"Yeah, Chem I AB." Ellen faked a shudder. "And dishwashing."

"Just think. No more workshifts. Five whole hours a week free to have fun."

"From what my sister tells me, we might be better off in the co-op washing our own dishes than here, washing—ugh—bedpans."

"Nurses don't have to do that much anymore, at least not nurses with college degrees."

"Not once we graduate and get a little experience," Ellen agreed. "I don't think I'd be here if I expected to be a floor nurse very long. But I suspect while we're students we'll still have to do some of the dirty work."

"Speaking of dirty work, how was your summer?"

Ellen held up small, soft hands. "See. No dirt under my nails."

"How did you manage that?"

"Well, if you must know the truth, I wore gloves. And I scrubbed a lot. No, seriously, Dad never did think girls should work in the fields. So I got a job at the Co-op Packing Shed."

"Somehow I'm not sure that's an improvement."

"Oh, but it is. It's a lot shadier; there's protection from the wind; it's even a little cleaner." She sighed. "Oh, Kim, can you imagine doing that sort of thing all your life—or even until you get married?"

"Working in Dad's store is bad enough!" Kim shook her head. "Speaking of marriage, did you manage to work things out with Ron?"

"There really wasn't anything more to work out, Kim. It's over. I like him a lot and always will, but we've outgrown each other." The words still hurt, but she insisted to herself that they were true. "We were high school sweethearts, but we're not in high school anymore."

"It's too bad. He's nice, Ellen, really nice."

"He's off to Texas to learn to fly airplanes. He's sure we'll be at war any day now, and he thinks he has to be part of it."

"Ellen, the news from Europe is bad. Germany has conquered almost everything but England already."

"So what? Oh, don't look so shocked. Mightn't it be better if Europe did just have one government, instead of all those little countries fighting among themselves all the time?"

"People say Hitler is a terrible man, Ellen. He wants

18

to kill all the Jews and the Slavs—anyone who isn't what he calls 'Aryan.'"

"You don't believe all those horror stories, do you? Surely the Germans would never elect a chancellor crazy enough to think he can kill people just because they look different."

Kim's dark eyes peered into Ellen's wide blue ones. "Maybe you can't believe it, Ellen, but I can. I'm a Nisei, remember? I was born in America, but my parents are still Japanese."

"Oh, come on. I know we haven't always been fair to you Japanese, but nobody's suggested killing you or even locking you up in ghettoes. And they never will. Not in this country. We aren't perfect, but we are civilized."

"We're civilized?" Kim took a framed photo from her suitcase and set it on the desk.

"Kim, I know you've had a harder time than I have, and I do want to understand. But what we have to do is get to know each other, not fight with each other. Your cousins are fighting my sister's friends in China, but look at how well we get along. So why can't the French and the Germans learn to live and let live for goodness sake?"

"Maybe someday." The girls unpacked in silence for a few minutes. "Say, Ellen, if you've really broken up with Ron, you'll be going to the mixer tomorrow night, won't you?"

"Tomorrow night? Well, if they don't see any point in wasting time, why should I? Sure. Where? What time? What shall we wear?"

The mixer was casual. Ellen would have liked to dress

19

up, to show off the slim, royal blue silk chemise she hadn't had a chance to wear all summer. But the navy pleated skirt and fluffy powder blue sweater set off her golden hair and hourglass figure. She danced at least once, it seemed, with every medical student in the room and with most of the new interns.

"Soledad?" they would ask, politely. "Just where is that?"

"A little bit south of Salinas. It's just a little farming town."

"Oh, yes. Salinas," her partner would respond. "Isn't that where John Steinbeck came from?"

"Don't mention Steinbeck!" She would shake her head in mock dismay. "Actually, my sister knew him when they were in high school. But *The Grapes of Wrath* is so overdone. It really wasn't that bad, even at its worst."

"I suppose not," he would shrug. Just then the band, a catch-up bunch of older med students who did a better Benny Goodman imitation than might have been expected, would slow down the beat. Ellen's partner would squeeze her just a little tighter. *If Dad had his way I'd still be square dancing.* The thought, and Ellen, would be swept away with the sweet strains of "Blueberry Hill."

Kim had fewer partners, Ellen noticed. It seemed natural to her that the Japanese students kept to themselves. But just who was that exceptionally handsome Nisei Kim was dancing with? He wasn't particularly tall, she thought, but so slender and lithe. He moved with an easy grace, even elegance.

She didn't have to wonder long. Kim steered the young man toward Ellen and her partner. As the music paused, Kim tapped Ellen's arm. "This is my brother, Kenji." She nudged him toward Ellen. "This is my roommate, Ellen."

He took her hand and smiled. "I've been hearing about you for two years, Ellen. I thought it was about time we met. Shall we dance?"

Ellen had never really looked at the Japanese who lived in the Salinas Valley. They were different; they didn't mingle. But as Kenji's arm circled her slender waist, Ellen studied her roommate's brother. His coal black hair was thick and lustrous, brushed cleanly back from a broad forehead; dark almond eyes sparkled under long black lashes. His cheek, as it brushed hers, was smooth and soft as a woman's, but his jaw was firm and strong.

And Kenji Ohata was not only very good-looking, but he was also a wonderful dancer. Ellen felt instantly at ease in his arms as he led her in the newest steps, steps he had not learned in the Salinas Valley, she suspected.

"I didn't know med students had time to take dancing lessons," she complimented as the music stopped. "But you didn't learn that in King City."

"Why not? We do have phonograph records and movies there, just like you do in Soledad." He led her to a small table. "Shall we sit this one out?"

"Kim told me she had a big brother here," Ellen said. "But she didn't tell me much more. Did you go to Cal too?"

"Yes, but I graduated the year before Kim started, so I missed meeting you there. She said you were pretty, and she was right about that. She said you were smart too. That's why I asked her to introduce us."

"So you're halfway through medical school." Ellen steered the conversation back to him; she knew young men didn't really want to talk about how smart girls were. "Is med school as hard as they say?"

He grinned. "If you survive the first year you've got it made, but oh, that first year. Watch out, though. Nursing school is like that too. They try to weed out the misfits early."

The music started again, and as he drew her back to the dance floor she noticed his hands. They were broad, strong, more like a farmer's hands than a surgeon's—a lot like Ron's, she realized. But what caught her attention was that they were as soft, and as carefully groomed, as her own. His touch, as he led the tango, was like his hands, strong and gentle at the same time. What was that he was saying?

"I didn't scare you, did I? Something tells me you're no misfit."

Oh, yes, nursing school. "I do know something about what I'm getting into," she assured him. "I have an older sister who's a nurse. She did it the old-fashioned way, but she encouraged me to go for my degree. I hope to go into public health."

"Good field. Less blood, and you don't lose so many patients. It doesn't pay a whole lot, but I guess a pretty girl like you doesn't have to worry much about that."

"Oh, you men. You all think we only work long enough to find husbands. My sister is married and has three kids, and she still works."

"Good for her. I hate to see talent wasted." He led her easily, in perfect time to the swing band. "Is she a public health nurse?"

"You might say so, but she doesn't work for the government. She's a Salvation Army officer."

If the music hadn't stopped he might have dropped her hand in astonishment. "Salvation Army? Your sister? I gather, considering your dancing ability, that you don't share her calling."

"Hardly," she rushed to assure him. "All that stuff about Jesus." She brushed it aside with a wave of her hand. "But she's really a good person, Kenji, and I admire her very much."

The music started, and he held her closely as they began to dance again. "It's Ken, by the way." His lips turned up in a smile but his eyes were suddenly sober. "All my friends call me that. I'm only Kenji to my family."

Chapter Three

*E*llen was trying to decide between a long strand of pearls and a chunky gold link necklace when Kim came in and dropped an armload of books on her bed. "Which do you think looks best with this sweater?" Ellen asked.

"Which do I think looks best, or which do I think Ken would like?" Kim answered. "Must be nice to be smart enough to go to the movies with final exams coming up next week."

"I can't study all the time. A good comedy relaxes me. We work hard all week and we need Saturday night off. Ken says the same thing."

"Ellen, I think we need to talk."

Kim sounded so serious. *Ron's mother, and now Kim.* "It isn't just finals, is it? Why don't you like me dating Ken? Don't you think I'm good enough for him?"

"Ellen, you know how much I like you, and I did want you and Kenji to be friends. I did introduce you, after all.

But you've scarcely seen anyone else all semester. I know several of the other med students have asked you out."

"And I've said yes a few times," Ellen reminded her. "I just happen to enjoy Ken's company more."

"Why?"

"He's stimulating. Ken makes me think."

"What you mean is that he's different, isn't it?"

"Heavens, no," Ellen insisted. "In fact, we're a lot alike. We like the same books, the same kind of movies. We both think the United States should stay out of this stupid war. And we both love to dance to a good swing band," she concluded, with a chuckle.

"Obviously he likes being with you, but . . ."

"Obviously. If he didn't, he'd quit asking me out."

"Ellen," Kim paused, as if searching for the right words. "I hope I'm not spreading tales, especially about my own brother, but you do know Ken's seeing other girls, don't you?"

"Sure." Ellen shrugged, but Kim's words disturbed her. "We're not serious. We just like doing things together."

"That's good, because it wouldn't work, Ellen." Kim shook her head. "I guess there's nothing wrong with your dating him here in San Francisco, but things are different at home. Have you ever thought of how your folks would react if Ken came to their house to pick you up for a date?"

"My folks aren't like that," she insisted. Actually, she had thought about it. *They wouldn't say anything. They'd be nice as pie, but afterward Mom would have a little talk with me and warn me not to get serious. Well, we're not serious, not yet anyhow.* "They liked you when we got together last summer," she reminded her friend.

"They were really nice that day, Ellen, to me and to my parents, but a college roommate is one thing. A Nisei boyfriend is quite another."

"Don't be silly. Anyhow, Ken isn't really my boyfriend." *Which is all too true,* she thought. Ken made no secret of the fact he was dating other girls, and even reminded her that she was free to date other men. "We just enjoy each other's company."

As she applied the rouge and lipstick her father still disapproved of, Ellen wondered why she was fascinated by Kenji Ohata. *Sure, he's different. Different from Soledad people, from Ron. He's an adult; he reads Hemingway and George Bernard Shaw. He isn't swept away by all this romantic war nonsense; he accepts people for what they are, not who their parents were or what church they go to.* She ran a comb quickly through her wavy hair as someone called for her from the foot of the stairs. *Besides, he's one of the best-looking men I've ever known, and he dances divinely.*

"You were right, as usual." Ellen was still laughing as they walked back to her dorm from the neighborhood movie theater. "Seeing *The Philadelphia Story* was so much better than trying to cram for exams—especially the part where Katharine Hepburn took that midnight swim!"

"She was terrific, wasn't she? But I can't figure out how she ever got engaged to that guy to begin with," Ken wondered. "He was the classic stuffed shirt if there ever were one."

"But it's such a typical rebound, Ken. Hepburn had to persuade herself, and everyone else, that she didn't still love Cary Grant. So she turned to someone who was his exact opposite."

"Women! Is it any wonder we don't understand you?" Ken feigned bewilderment. "Brrr, it's cold. How about a cup of coffee?"

They stepped inside a little cafe. It was busy with other after-movie snackers, but Ken found an empty booth. "So, Ellen, is that why you date me?" he asked. "Is it because I'm so different from the boy back home?"

"Oh, don't be silly," she protested. "Ron and I grew up together, but that was just a high school romance."

"Kim said it was pretty serious when she first knew you. What happened, Ellen? Or isn't it any of my business?"

"There's no big secret, Ken. Ron was a football player; his family has a farm near ours; we all went to the same church. Of course, I thought I was madly in love when I was seventeen. All girls do."

"Like Midori and me," he commented.

"Midori?"

"My high school sweetheart," he confessed. "She's in nurses' training in San Jose now. She's a sweet kid, but . . ."

"And Ron's a swell guy. I guess I went to Cal mostly to be with him," she admitted, "but then we changed. We grew up." *You aren't supposed to talk about old beaux on a date*, she thought. *But Ken is so easy to talk to.* "At least I grew up. Ron's still a Soledad farmer at heart, and he's definitely still a Soledad Methodist. Ken," she asked soberly, "do you know anyone else, anyone from our generation, with a good education, who still believes God created the world in six days?"

"I don't know many people who believe in God at all," Ken told her. "My folks observe the teachings of Buddha, more or less, and honor their ancestors, but this Christian idea of God being involved directly in people's lives seems rather farfetched to me."

She nodded. "That's what I mean. Ron can't seem to see that the Bible is just a good book, and Jesus was just a great teacher. If people would do as Jesus taught this would be a good world, but instead they make him a God. They cling to a lot of outdated myths, and if you dare to disagree with them, you're going to hell. Well, I'm as good as they are, and I'm not going to hell."

Kenji smiled at her defensive outburst. "We don't believe in hell, except maybe hell on earth. Some Japanese believe in reincarnation—you keep coming back until you get it right. Personally I think once is enough."

"Doesn't that depend?" She chuckled softly. "I wonder if life is really such a wonderful gift for some people, but you? Just look at you. You're handsome and smart. You know how to have a good time. And you're on your way to being a successful doctor."

"Don't get me wrong, Ellen. I'm grateful to be alive, and I intend to get everything out of life that I can. But one day I'll get old—if the war lets me—and sick, and then I'd just as soon get out of it all. No, the eternal life Christians talk about just doesn't appeal to me."

"You agree with the people who say hell is right here on earth. Well, I think heaven's here, too, or could be. If we each do right by our own conscience, live at peace with our fellow men and women, and help one another, we can make the world a better place and find happiness for ourselves too. The human race has evolved this far already. Why can't everyone see how much further we can go?"

"I don't know, but it's too late to figure it out tonight." Ken looked at his watch. "You'll miss lock-out, and that won't do much for your noble goals."

At the door Ken took her lightly in his arms and touched his lips to hers. Her blood raced at the earthy touch, casual though it was. Ron had seldom touched her so intimately, even in the old days, when they'd been so sure they were in love. Ellen told herself the kiss meant nothing to Ken—not yet, anyhow. "Thanks for the break, Ken," she whispered. "I had a grand time."

Kim was asleep, or seemed to be, so Ellen undressed quietly in the dark. She thought not about the heaven on earth she'd discussed with Ken, but of heaven on earth à la Hollywood. She smiled as she recalled the Jimmy Stewart role, the shy, well-meaning reporter of *The Philadelphia Story*. Stewart reminded her, she realized, of Ron. *Good, down-to-earth, lots of common sense. Never think of insulting a girl by giving her a casual kiss; wouldn't even get close enough to dance with her; always the perfect gentleman.* As she snuggled into the covers she remembered Ron's perpetual propriety. *Even Jimmy Stewart had slipped, but Ron never would,* she assured herself. *He was just so incredibly dull.*

Ken was more the Cary Grant type. A little shiver of excitement rippled through her body, as she imagined Ken sweeping her off her feet and dragging her to the altar. *I could do a lot worse. He does have a great future, and he's mature and alive and exciting.*

A little voice in the back of her mind whispered a reminder. *He isn't serious. He's still seeing other girls.* But if Ken gave kisses lightly, Ellen hadn't learned to take them that way. *He's probably just holding back because he thinks I wouldn't marry a Japanese. He knows he's as good as anyone else, but he thinks it would be hard for me.* Ken excited her, and if Kim were right and the fascination of the exotic was all it was, Ellen wasn't about to admit that, even to herself. *I'll just have to try to show him that it doesn't matter to me. So what if his parents happened to come from Japan.*

She wriggled deep into the covers and fell asleep imagining the scene at home when she told Mom and Dad that she was going to marry this enchanting Nisei.

Chapter Four

The school year had flown by with its lectures and ward rounds. Ellen and Kim took the train down to the Salinas Valley together for a two-week vacation, before the summer session and their first real hospital training.

"I'm so excited about actually starting to do some nursing," Kim said, as she settled into her seat for the trip. "But it will be good to get home for a few days first."

"I'm going to sleep the clock around the first week," Ellen vowed. "I'm sure the family has all kinds of plans, but I'm so sick of getting up for eight o'clock classes. Besides, I suspect we're in for a busy two months. Diet kitchen, operating room, out-patient clinics, medical and surgical wards! Whew!"

"The diet kitchen shouldn't take long." Kim shrugged. "But just think, our first time in the operating room. That's what I've been waiting for."

"My sister always liked it, though of course she does mostly clinic stuff now."

"She met her husband in OR, didn't she?"

"Yes, he was a brilliant surgeon until his hands were injured in a fire. He can do just about anything else with them, but he's pretty much had to give up surgery."

"It's kind of funny, isn't it?"

"What?"

"Your sister being a Salvation Army missionary in China, and you saying you don't even believe in God. When I first met you I thought this was my big chance to find out what Christianity was all about, but your religion doesn't mean any more to you than mine does to me."

"My folks are religious enough. They took me to Sunday school and the Methodist church all my life. But it never 'took' with me like it did with Marianne. She was sick for a long time when she was a teenager—TB. I guess that's when she 'got religion,' really. After that she joined the Salvation Army, and she met Paul, and they went off to save China."

"Well, it's a long ride to Soledad, and I'm still curious. So tell me, what do Christians believe that Buddhists, say, don't? What made your sister go to China? What did Ron believe that was so important it broke you two up?"

Ellen thought she'd put that behind her, but Kim's question about Ron still rubbed a tender spot deep inside her. "There are lots of myths in the Bible, Kim, like the story about Jonah and the whale, or the walls of Jericho falling down when the people shouted."

"So, every culture has myths."

"People like Ron don't think they're myths. He insists they really happened. And he insists Jesus is really God, and that he rose from the dead."

"And if a person really believes that—can believe that—" Kim said, almost wistfully, "it has to make religion the most important thing in his life."

"Sure, and it also makes him narrow-minded and intolerant," Ellen snapped.

"How can you say that? Everyone in your whole family is a believer, and they're good people."

The sharpness of Ellen's own words had shocked her. She thought of the loved ones she would be seeing again soon—Gran, who was always kind to everyone and Carrie and Matt Hanlon, who had taken her in as a baby and raised her in their own love-filled home. "Yes," she agreed. "And if all Christians lived like they do—loved their neighbors, did to others as they would have others do to them—I'd be as good a Christian as anybody."

Kim nodded. "If Christians followed Jesus, and Buddhists followed Buddha, and Moslems followed Mohammed, the world wouldn't be about to blow itself up."

They fell silent, then, turning to their own thoughts as the train chugged south. *Yes, many of the Christians she knew were wonderful people*, Ellen told herself. *Most of them.* And if the word *noble* could ever be used honestly, it described her sister, Marianne, and her husband, no matter what the whispering old hens hinted.

But those women claimed to be Christians, too, and they said such terrible things about Marianne—and about me too. Ellen tried to shut the gossip out of her memory. *But what if it were true? It would explain a lot of things: why Carrie and Matt took me in; why Marianne, who says she was my mother's friend, always evades my questions; why Dad has always been so strict with me. Is he afraid I'll get in trouble, too, like my mother did? No, it just couldn't be true. They wouldn't live that kind of a lie.*

And Ron? How could I call him narrow-minded and intolerant? Sure, he broke up with me, but he's never turned against me.

She thought of Ron's latest letter. He was still in Texas. He wrote, with a touch of pride, that he had won his wings and was ready for the fight whenever it came. But he did not want war, she knew. Ron really believed that Hitler intended to destroy the decent world he believed in, and was convinced this war was the only way to preserve freedom. *But Ron doesn't want to kill people any more than I do, any more than Ken does.*

"Kenji's coming down next weekend, isn't he?" she asked Kim as the train chugged down the peninsula.

"Yes, he is. He's working over the Fourth of July, so he got this Friday off. Why?"

"Oh, I thought it might be fun if we all got together."

"All who?"

"Ken, me, you, some of your friends, some of my cousins."

Kim seemed uncertain. "Ellen, you and I and Ken and some other med student is fine. But our friends and your cousins? Do you really think that's a good idea?"

"As a matter of fact, I think it's a very good idea, Kim. I'm sure they'd like each other, if they just had a chance to get acquainted."

She said the same thing to her mother the next Saturday afternoon, when Carrie asked the same question.

"How much did you tell Sammy about this 'friend' of yours when you set up this double date?" Carrie asked.

"Now, Mom, I told him she was cute, which she is, and lots of fun to be with, which she is. If you mean did I tell him she was Japanese, why should I? What does it matter?"

"Ellen, you know your father and I believe the Japanese are good people. They are honest and hardworking. They don't make trouble. But they aren't like us. They keep to themselves, and we keep to ourselves. It's just better that way."

"Kim is a wonderful friend, Mother, and I've been dating Ken all winter. We double-date a lot in San Francisco, so why not here?"

"Things are different there, and I'm not at all sure it's for the better. People may be more used to that sort of thing up in the city. Those are all college people. Your cousin Sam isn't. He's a Soledad farmer. I don't say it's right to think that way, but to Sam, Japanese are field hands."

"Ken will be a doctor in a year. Kim will be a nurse, just like me. Their father runs a grocery store."

"I know, I know," Carrie protested. "But you have to understand other people's feelings too."

"Trust me. Once Sam meets Kim he'll think she's a swell girl, and we'll all have a great evening."

"I hope you're right, and it's only an evening out after all. Where are you going, by the way?"

"Just dinner and a show, Mom." Ellen knew Sam would tell his folks the same thing. Not that Will and Irene McLean objected to their son's going dancing, but

Matt Hanlon, Ellen's father, was, as she and Sam had agreed, such an old fuddy-duddy. "You'd think he'd trust me just a little," Ellen had often grumbled. But just getting him to the point of accepting movies had been tough enough. Dancing was still taboo.

Carrie was right about Salinas Valley people, Ellen admitted. Even being in Ken's arms on the dance floor didn't seem right that night. No one in the little King City restaurant had given them a second glance when she and Sam came in the door, but then they joined Ken and Kim at the booth in the corner. The young waitress was not even subtle as she passed them by, busily taking orders from everyone else until Ken had called to her. Eyebrows raised as people at other tables noticed the foursome.

And Sam had not really helped. *I guess maybe I should have warned him after all*, Ellen conceded to herself. *But did he have to stand there with his mouth open for ten minutes? Maybe not ten minutes, but it seemed like it.* He had taken the seat next to Kim, though, and smiled gamely. By the time they had eaten, he and Kim were chatting like old friends.

But then they had driven over to the Legion Hall. The middle-aged man at the door glowered at them. "What are you kids doing here?"

"I thought your dances were open to the public," Ken had answered coolly.

"I don't know you kids, and I don't want any trouble."

"Neither do we. We like to dance, and we thought this would be a good place to have some clean fun." Ellen had never heard Ken sound like this. His voice was calm, but measured. Where was the bantering tone and easy self-confidence she was used to? Now he seemed to be weighing each word, being much too careful, too polite, almost servile, she realized.

"Did we misunderstand?" she found herself asking. "If the dances aren't open to the public . . ."

"We could just go to a show," Sam offered.

But Ken persisted, respectfully but firmly. "My sister and I live here, and these are college friends who happen to live up in Soledad. If we aren't welcome, we will leave, but I always thought the Legion had dances to raise money, and we did buy tickets."

The legionnaire didn't seem happy, but he did take the proffered tickets and step aside. The hall was full. King City young people were out of school for the summer. Several, like Ellen's group, were home from college. Young farmers were taking a welcome break between planting and harvest. And aside from a local movie theater, the Legion dances were about the only place to take a nice girl on a Saturday night date.

Ellen wished they had a live band, but at least they had lots of the latest records, and they kept the music coming—Glenn Miller, Benny Goodman, the Dorseys. Sam was being nice to Kim, though it did look like he was deliberately keeping to the dimly lit edge of the crowded dance floor.

Not Ken! They were a well-matched pair, Ellen knew, and they had been dancing together all winter. It was only natural that people would notice as Ken swung her gracefully away from him and then back into his arms. But second glances turned to stares. Other couples moved aside; girls excused themselves; and men gathered in little knots. And Ellen knew what they were thinking.

Most of the girls returned to their partners, and most of the couples began dancing again. But the undercurrent was there; Ellen felt it. She was used to hearing whispers, but not this kind. "Japs don't belong here." "How'd they get in?" "What kind of white kids would go out with them anyhow?"

Ken pretended not to hear or see. Ellen, who had never felt uncomfortable in his arms before, was angry. *Does everybody in this insufferable valley whisper about everybody else?* she raged inwardly. When they joined Sam and Kim for Cokes she whispered, "What's the matter with these people? What have we ever done to them?"

"I'm sorry, Ellen. I should have expected trouble," Ken said softly. "I've been to these dances before, but not with a white girl. I guess that's the problem."

"Maybe we should just leave," Sam suggested. "I'm sure none of us is having that much fun." He glanced at his date. "Not that you aren't a swell girl, Kim, but . . ."

A few feet away Ellen heard a rowdy voice. "Well, I'm not going to let a couple of Japs spoil my night. Anybody coming with me?"

A handful of young men broke away from the group and approached Ken. "Look," one of them snarled. "We don't want any trouble, so why don't you just get out of here and quit spoiling the party."

Ken glanced at the two girls, took Ellen's arm, and began to move toward the door. Surprisingly, it was Sam who spoke up. "We don't want any trouble either, so why don't you mind your own business?"

The dancers began to move off the floor, circling the hall nervously. Kim tugged Sam's sleeve and begged him to just leave. Ken shook his head in warning. But the older legionnaire who was playing the records picked up a megaphone. "Come on, folks. I've got some great platters here, and the night's young. Let's dance!"

Young men in suits and ties looked at young women in dirndl skirts and peasant blouses, twisting lacy hand-kerchiefs. The young men shifted uneasily from foot to foot. A few of the girls pulled their young men back onto the dance floor. The girls from the nearby cluster re-claimed their partners. "Come on, they really aren't doing anything. He's right. Let's dance."

The incident was over. "Let's dance," Ken said to Ellen, as Sam took Kim loosely in his arms. But after that dance, they quietly slipped out.

Sam dropped Ken and Kim at their house a few blocks away, then headed home in stony silence.

"What's the matter, Sam?" Ellen asked after a few awkward moments.

"Ellen, why did you do that?"

"Do what?"

She feigned innocence, but Sam was not about to be put off. "Set up a date like that?" he snapped.

"But Kim's a nice girl, Sam. She's my best friend. She . . ."

"She's a nice girl, but Ellen, for crying out loud, they're Japs. Maybe people do things like that up in the big city, but here we like to keep to our own kind."

"I just thought if we could get to know each other better we'd find out how much alike we are. Sam, it isn't right, this living next door to people and not knowing them or being afraid of them because we don't understand them. That's why we fight, why we have wars."

"Look, you're probably right, but that's not the real world. You think because you went off to college and listened to all those hoity-toity professors and read all those books that you have all the answers. Well, people here think differently. My folks have one of the biggest and best farms in the valley. McLean Farms ships out the best lettuce in the country. My folks are good, God-fearing people, and their ways are plenty good enough for me."

"Sam, I love Uncle Will and Aunt Irene. And Mom and Dad are wonderful parents, the best I could ever wish for. But that doesn't mean they're perfect. That doesn't mean we have to be just like them."

"They're good enough for Ron too," Sam muttered. "Guess that's why you two broke up. Sure hard to figure why you'd give up a great guy like Ron for a Jap, though."

"He's not a Jap," she snapped. "He's as American as you or I." *Besides*, she almost said, *it was Ron who broke up with me. He's just too much of a gentleman to make me look bad.* She sat beside her cousin and watched the moonlit fields slip by for several minutes. "Thank you, Sam," she said at last. "Thank you for sticking up for them, anyhow."

Chapter Five

*E*llen had hoped to see Ken often during the busy summer session. But the forty-four hours a week she spent on the surgical and medical wards left little time and even less energy for movies or dancing, anyhow, she rationalized. And Ken was working full time as an orderly. *Still, you'd think he would at least call.*

"Surely he hasn't been avoiding me just because of that little incident in June," she said to Kim one evening.

"We were all lucky that 'little incident' didn't turn into a brawl. If Ken hadn't worked hard to keep his temper, and if that legionnaire hadn't been quick with his tongue . . ."

"But that was just a few punks, Kim. It wasn't Ken's fault."

"He knows that, Ellen. But he still feels bad that you and your cousin were embarrassed." Kim frowned. "By the way, you shouldn't have caught your cousin off guard like that. Sam's nice, and he didn't deserve to be put on the spot."

"I didn't think it would matter. And it shouldn't have, either."

"But it does."

Ellen was uneasy. She and Kim seldom discussed Kim's race. *To me*, she insisted to herself, *it doesn't matter. And it shouldn't to Sam.* "Sam was on your side," she protested.

"Sam tried to make the best of a bad situation. I do appreciate the way he talked back to those guys, but if you hadn't maneuvered him into it Sam McLean would never have dated me. I know you meant well, but it would have been better if he never had. Ken knows it too. Ken likes you, Ellen, and he hated seeing you hurt."

"If I was embarrassed it was for the other guys, not Ken. He was a gentleman the whole time. Kim, I don't care that he's Japanese any more than I care that you are."

Still, Ken hadn't asked her out all summer. *Maybe if we had a chance to talk it over*, she had told herself. *Surely Ken can see how perfect we are together. After all, if we got married we wouldn't be living in the Salinas Valley.*

Not that she had any reason to think of marriage to Ken, she knew. He'd never implied their relationship was anything more than companionship. *But when I'm with him I feel so alive, and I know he does too. He's so much more intense, and, yes, more challenging, than Ron ever was. We could have a really good life together*, she told herself. *We could make all these back-water bigots see how wrong they are.*

Now Ellen was on her way to Soledad. She had planned to stay in San Francisco during the semester break. But Marianne had come home, and Ellen wanted to spend the precious few days with her oldest sister. As her train chugged through the familiar towns of the peninsula Ellen's heart ached for Marianne, who had spent all her life helping people. Now she had been forced to bring her small children home, leaving her husband, Paul, behind in China.

"I'm so afraid for Paul," Marianne had written. "We hear terrible stories from the coast, where the Japanese are in control. They show no mercy, especially to Westerners. But Paul doesn't feel he can leave our people, and we pray the Lord will protect him. Meanwhile, he insists I take the children to safety."

Her train pulled into San Jose. Ellen squirmed uneasily, recalling her last talk with Kim. When she had looked at her roommate's dark, tilted eyes and straight black hair, somehow, just for an instant, Kim had looked different.

"My sister's bringing her children home because of the war in China," Ellen had explained briefly. "I guess things are pretty awful there."

Kim nodded. "She's afraid of the Japanese army, isn't she? I've read a few stories in the newspaper, about the rape of Nanking—things like that."

"I'm sure the Chinese army isn't any better," Ellen offered. "But they have heard that women and children have been badly treated. And then there are food shortages, and the shelling and bombing."

"My father doesn't believe most of the horror stories, Ellen. He grew up in Japan. They always thought of the

Chinese as enemies, and he isn't surprised that the Japanese took advantage of the revolution to invade. But we're not beasts, Ellen. The Japanese people love peace and beauty. Those stories about Japanese soldiers butchering innocent people just have to be lies."

Well, Marianne and her children will be safe, at least, Ellen thought, as the train rattled on toward home. And Paul was an American. The Japanese wouldn't dare harm him deliberately. If they captured the town he was in, they would just send him home, she assured herself.

Marianne had been home for over a week, but Carrie waited to have the big family dinner until Ellen could be there too. "Thank God," Marianne had whispered as the sisters set the long table. "I needed a little time to unwind before the family reunion. There are just so many of us. Besides, everything is so strange to the kids."

"Where are they, anyhow? They're so quiet I'd scarcely know they were in the house."

"They're out 'helping' Grandpa feed the chickens." Marianne laughed. It was the first time Ellen had heard Marianne's infectious chuckle, so like her own, since she got home. "Chickens, at least, are familiar to them, Ellen. Do you realize that their father and I are virtually the only Americans they've ever known? Their nursemaid, their playmates, the shopkeepers, all Chinese. For me, it's easy. When I walk up these front steps I feel like I'm a little girl again, back home, even though I haven't been here in five years."

Ellen began folding napkins and laying them next to the familiar willowware plates. "It doesn't seem like it's been that long. I remember helping you bandage up the migrant workers' kids. That's when I decided to become a nurse."

"Well, you're on your way now." Ellen saw warm approval in her sister's deep turquoise eyes. "I'm so proud of you going for a degree too. I wish I'd had that kind of education. I could have done so much more. Of course, Paul has taught me a lot."

They heard Matt Hanlon come into the kitchen with his little trail of helpers. Their eager questions came in a garbled mix of English and Chinese, and Marianne smiled again as she heard her son rephrase them for their grandfather. "Yes, Mark is the only one of my children who even remembers California. Jade was only a year old when we went back to China after our furlough, and Pearl's never been here at all."

The family began arriving: Uncle Will and Aunt Irene, with Sam, Joe, and Beth; Uncle Tim and Aunt Nancy and their three. The cousins had grown up with Ellen. Marianne, fifteen years older, was almost a stranger to them.

Marianne and Ellen's brother, Ted, and his wife had stopped out in the yard, where their two youngsters were getting acquainted with their cousins from China. Liz, the sister between Ted and Ellen, would be along later.

Ellen glanced out the bay window. Her Uncle Harry was helping his mother out of the car. "There's Gran."

"She's aged so," Marianne murmured.

"Yes. I noticed when I came home in June, but even the past two months I'm afraid she's failing."

At the table, Anna motioned to Marianne and Ellen

to take the seats on either side of her. "I want my big girl and my little girl next to me, here," she said softly. The room was so noisy, though, that one more conversation was too much effort for the old woman. She seemed content just to look down the long table and see her family together and happy.

But Ellen felt sorry for Marianne's children, sitting out in the kitchen with their cousins and cousins once-removed, family, but strangers. *Getting this family straightened out is too much even for a grown-up.*

Ellen smiled as she practiced an imaginary introduction. *This is Gran. Her name is Anna McLean, and she is Sam McLean's widow (that's old Sam McLean the first). Carrie, my mother, and Uncle Will and Uncle Tim are Sam's by his first wife. Harry and Adele are Sam and Anna's kids . . .*

Of course, the imaginary explanation might go on, if the details really mattered, if she were explaining the complicated family tree to Ken, say. *I'm not blood kin to any of them. Mom and Dad, that's Matt and Carrie Hanlon, adopted me. My mother was a friend of Marianne's who died.* That was all they had told her. She had asked questions, but they always brushed them aside.

Ellen did not let herself think about her biological parents very often. The Hanlons and McLeans had love enough to share, and she tried not to think about being "adopted." Even when she overheard a few words of the ugly gossip she refused to think of it as anything but one more proof of the small-town mentality she despised.

Still, when Marianne was around, she could not help wondering. *Maybe now I'll get a chance to talk to her about my real mother,* Ellen thought. *Surely she'll understand I need to know the truth. And if the gossip is true.* Ellen looked at the woman across the table and almost hoped it was true. *I do love Mom and Dad*, she told herself, *but is it wrong to want to know who I really am?*

The menfolk were talking, as McLean and Hanlon men always did when they got together, about the crops. As usual, Ellen was bored. "Sometimes," she said to Marianne, "I wonder if they know there's a world out there beyond the hills."

"They know," Marianne answered with a smile. "Who do you think buys the lettuce?" She paused. "It's the same in China, you know, although there the talk about crops is more urgent somehow. Here, it's profits; there, it's getting enough rice to stave off starvation."

"I guess it is kind of silly of me. Of course, food is important. But if we didn't waste so much effort on war, wouldn't we have plenty for everybody, even in China?"

"Maybe," Marianne conceded. "But I think you're asking more than mankind, on its own, can ever achieve. Greed is universal, Ellen. For some people, maybe most people, enough is never enough."

Ellen shook her head. "No, back during the Depression we had some hungry people around here, and we had riots and stuff. Now everybody's working again, and everything's back to normal. I know the Bible says everybody's naturally wicked, but then why does the Salvation Army work so hard to feed people and get them jobs, if you don't expect them to be better people afterward?"

"You're forgetting the most important ingredient, Ellen. Food and shelter and jobs are peripherals. It is Jesus that makes the difference. We believe our good works make people more willing to listen to the gospel, but it is the gospel that makes them better people. Even Paul and I are missionaries first and medical workers second."

One of the cousins interrupted from across the table. "But you will be staying here in Soledad for a while, won't you, Marianne? At least until Paul comes home?"

"I'm not sure. I'm still an officer in the Salvation Army, so like any soldier I go where I'm told. Paul could have come back with me, you know. He was given the choice, but he felt his first duty was to the people in the villages, just as he insisted mine was to the children."

"It must be terrible for you, though, worrying about him over there," her cousin sympathized. "What do you think the Japs would do if they caught him?"

"Wouldn't they just order him out of the country, Marianne?" Ellen asked. "Surely the horror stories we've heard are exaggerations."

"I'm sure a lot of them are," Marianne agreed. "That's what we told ourselves in China, too, but some of it is true. The goal of the present Japanese government is to control all of Asia, I'm afraid. And to do that they are bent on driving out all westerners."

"Then Paul should have left with you," another cousin protested.

"I wish he had," Marianne admitted, "but the people in our villages do know us and trust us. I can only pray that they, and God, will keep Paul safe."

Even Ellen joined in the quiet "amen" that echoed around the long dining room table.

Six days later Ellen was packing in the upstairs room

that had been hers all her life. Before that it had been Marianne's, and this week they had shared it. Ellen heard steps on the stairs and turned to see her sister's smiling face. Marianne had a letter in her hand "My orders have come," she said. "Looks like we'll be seeing quite a bit of each other. I've been assigned to the Chinatown Corps again."

"Oh, that's wonderful." Ellen hugged her warmly. "Will you be nursing there?"

"Oh, yes. There's a little clinic for the poor, and I used to do a lot of home nursing—visiting nurse type of thing—when I worked there years ago with my friend Jade. You'll have to come down and help now and then." She chuckled softly. "On your free time, of which I'm sure you'll have plenty."

Ellen laughed too. "Well, we do get a little," she admitted. "But I'll have thirty hours a week of ward work this year, plus thirteen hours of lecture and all the study that goes with it."

"We worked fifty-five-hour weeks when I trained, and we studied when we could find odd moments."

"Oh, I know it used to be harder, Marianne, but did you have quizzes every week, and mid-term exams, and finals?"

"I wish we had." Ellen stared at her as Marianne explained. "When I was a nursing student we learned what we could, mostly by asking questions or, if we were lucky, by borrowing some of the doctors' books. We were as well trained, basically, as we wanted to be. It's been less than twenty years, but there have been a lot of changes. And all for the best."

"Then you don't think I'm being selfish taking the

long way and getting my bachelor's degree? I could have gone to a three-year school and had my R.N. by now."

Marianne didn't hesitate. "Absolutely not! The more you learn the more use you can be. And it's better for you too. You've studied history, literature, languages. You've learned enough basic science so that you'll know not only what to do, but why. Knowledge is good, Ellen, always."

"It's funny, in a way, that you should say that. I'm not sure Mom and Dad agree."

"Come on, now. Of course, they do."

"Mom was shocked when I asked her after church this morning if she really believed God created the world out of nothing in six days. I should think you, with all your religion, would disapprove of modern science."

"I do disapprove of some science teachers, Ellen, the ones who lack faith in anything but themselves. But facts, real facts, can't hurt anyone. It's what we do with them that counts."

"There's so much proof, Marianne. So much scientific data contradicts the Bible. So how can we believe any of it?"

"Ellen, I don't know how long it took God to create the earth, and I don't think it matters, though he certainly could have done it in six days."

"Then where did the fossils come from?" Ellen interrupted.

"Maybe God created fossils." Marianne shrugged. "I don't have all the answers, but neither do your teachers, Ellen. You can't accept everything they say at face value. Consider it; weigh it; and, yes, pray over it. Remember, God's Word has been around a lot longer than your science teachers. And God's Word has the answers to the questions that really matter."

"Sometimes I wish you'd at least put up an argument," Ellen chided. "In a way I'd like to believe the way you do, the way I did when I was little, but . . ."

"Lunch is ready," their mother called from downstairs.

"We'll have lots of chances to talk again, Ellen."

Ellen was glad Marianne would be nearby. *She's naive, in a way, but she's always so sure about everything. She's so completely confident, and yet she doesn't judge. Besides, maybe in San Francisco, without Mom around, I'll have a chance to talk to her about my real mother.*

Chapter Six

The war seemed to be coming closer that fall of 1941, since Hitler had invaded his one-time ally, Russia. Some of her old friends in the anti-war movement had changed their tune now, as Ron had pointed out in his last letter. But Ellen still hoped Roosevelt would go no further than his Lend-Lease program. *At least most of those kids agree with me about that,* she thought.

She was thinking of the handful of young interns she had gone out with since Ken had been so studiously avoiding her. They all seemed so shallow. All they could talk about was the World Series or how their old college football teams were doing, or how much money they would make when they got into practice.

Then, out of the blue, Ken had called. *Maybe he's finally decided to ignore that silly thing in King City,* she thought, humming brightly to herself as she primped for their first date in months. *And a tea dance at the Palace Hotel. This is an occasion.*

"Mail's here," Kim announced, tossing a letter on Ellen's dresser. "Postmarked Tacoma, Washington. Who do you know up there?"

"Nobody," Ellen puzzled, picking up the envelope. She recognized the bold handwriting, though. "It's from Ron." She opened it and scanned the two short pages. "He's been transferred to an air base there. They're learning to fly some new bomber." She shuddered. "Even Ron says he hopes they never have to use them."

"I'm glad you still write back and forth, Ellen. You and he always seemed so right for each other."

"Well, we're not," she snapped, a little too quickly. "Not that way, anyhow. But when you've known someone all your life it's only natural to keep in touch." Sometimes it did puzzle Ellen, though. Most guys, when they broke off with a girl, didn't keep teasing her with letters, even casual, brotherly letters. *Probably still hoping to convert me*, she decided. But she treasured the letters, nonetheless.

When Ken came, she laid the letter on her dresser, gave her hair a final quick brushing, put on a perky bright blue velvet beret, and went downstairs.

"Oh, this is wonderful," she breathed as they danced together in the sunlit Garden Court. She realized that some eyes had turned as they twirled on the crowded dance floor, and she did overhear a whisper or two, but people who went to tea dances at the Palace Hotel did not make ugly scenes. "See, we can have good times together, Ken. Civilized people don't make a fuss over nothing."

The music stopped and he guided her to a small table. "I guess I should confess. I think that's why I had to bring you here, just once, just to prove I could."

"Just once," she protested. "Of course I know it's terribly expensive, but someday, when you're a successful doctor . . ."

"That isn't what I mean." His meticulously manicured fingers drummed the table. "Ellen, I needed to talk to you. I owe you, at least, an explanation. We can't go on like this."

"I know. I've missed you all summer," she told him. "You've been so distant since King City. Don't you know it doesn't matter what people think as long as we like being together?"

"I think it does, or at least it would, eventually." He paused. His look was more tender than she had seen before, yet his black eyes burned intensely. "Ellen, this won't work. I like you—a lot. I think you like me, too, maybe too much. That's why we have to stop seeing each other."

She felt the beat of the big band vibrating across the dance floor. *Bewitched, Bothered and Bewildered*, the words echoed in her mind. She refused to listen to Ken's words. "Don't be silly. Come on, let's dance some more."

He took her hand, and led her onto the floor, but as they danced he continued to speak. "It's like the song, Ellen. You're bewitched, and so, I guess, am I. We're each enchanted by the world the other represents. But for us it isn't love, not the kind of love that lasts. And even if it were . . ."

"But it is, Ken," she interrupted. "It is for me, and I

think it is for you." *Well,* she argued with herself, *isn't it? Doesn't he feel it, too, this electricity. If he doesn't, why are we here together?*

His hand guided her gracefully away from him. She twirled lightly to the upbeat rhythm, and danced back into his arms. But he held her loosely, at arms' length, until the music stopped, and then led her from the floor.

"Ellen, it won't be easy for me, running into you on campus and hearing about you all the time from Kim, but I'm not going to ask you out again."

She sensed that it was virtually a vow. She also realized, shocked, that Ron had used almost the same words, and the same tone. "But Ken . . ."

"I mean it, Ellen. We have no future together. There are too many obstacles. This has to end, now, while I still have the willpower to end it."

"But it doesn't have to end," she protested.

"I'm afraid it does. Our backgrounds, our families, even the law."

"The law?"

"Ellen, surely you're aware that even if we were willing to face all the other difficulties, we could never marry. This is California. It's against the law."

"That's ridiculous. This is twentieth-century America. How could it be against the law?"

"Nonetheless, it is," he assured her. "Did you honestly not know there was a law on the books in this state forbidding marriage between Caucasians and Orientals?"

He stood and offered her his hand. "I'm taking you back to the dorm now. Please, Ellen, let this thing between us go, before it hurts us both more than we've already been hurt."

She was too stunned by his words to resist. And he was true to his word. He did not call again. He avoided her, overtly, obviously. Kim seemed a part of his plan, too, scarcely mentioning her brother and turning Ellen's questions aside with monosyllables.

Ellen shared Thanksgiving dinner with Marianne in her small Chinatown flat. The rooms were sparsely furnished, but crowded with childish laughter. It was raining outside, but warm and sunny with love inside. *And Marianne was so easy to talk to,* Ellen thought, *on most subjects at least.*

"So he broke it off," Ellen explained sadly. "But it isn't fair. Marianne, in this day and age, how can there be such a law? If we love each other, nothing else should matter."

"Love is a wonderful thing—the most wonderful thing God has given us. But life isn't like the movies, Ellen. Two people can be very much in love, and still the obstacles may be too great."

"We could go to another state."

"Yes, but that wouldn't change the other things." Marianne hesitated. "I'm sorry you've been hurt, but I can't help but think Ken is right about this."

"You agree with the family, don't you? I thought you'd be different, living in China all those years, having close friends who were Chinese. But you're just as prejudiced as the others."

"I hope I'm not, Ellen. The best friend I ever had was Chinese, though there were people who disapproved even of our friendship. But marriage is more difficult. You can't build a marriage alone; families do count, in the long run. And what about children? Would you want your children to be outcasts?"

"The families would come around. If Mom and Dad knew Ken, they'd love him, too, and I know I could win over his parents. Kim and I are already close, after all. And as for our children, the people who count will accept them—the good, decent, intelligent people. Moving back east would probably make that easier too."

"I doubt it," Marianne answered. "No, the world you want is a good one. It just isn't real, not now anyway. Ken seems to know that, and to care enough about you to accept that reality. I know you're hurt right now. It's all right to be hurt. But eventually . . ."

". . . I'll find the right person, and I'll realize this was all for the best," Ellen finished, bitterly. "But I'll never believe it was all for the best. How can it be best that two people who love each other, who have so much in common, who are so good together, should be kept apart because one of them happens to have Japanese parents?" She brushed at her tears. "How can it matter that his parents were Japanese, when I don't even know who my parents were?"

Marianne stiffened. "Would you go see what the kids are doing, please, while I finish stripping the meat off this turkey carcass?"

Ellen complied, but when she returned she confronted her sister. "Marianne, every time I bring up my mother, my *real* mother, you manage to change the subject."

Marianne screwed down the lid on the mayonnaise jar she had filled with turkey scraps. "She's dead."

"I know, but who was she? What was she like? What was her name? What did she look like? What did she think about things?"

"She was very young, Ellen." Marianne said the words as if by rote, avoiding Ellen's eyes as she spoke. "She was sick, and I only knew her for a few weeks, in the hospital."

Why does she always do that when I ask about my mother? Ellen thought. *Well, this time I'm going to get answers*, she resolved. "Marianne, I'm a woman, now, and I think it's time I knew the truth." Her sister concentrated on filling the dishpan. "I love you, Marianne and I don't want anyone hurt. I just want the truth."

Marianne spoke without looking up. "If you don't want anyone hurt, let the past alone."

"How can I? Marianne, I know Mom and Dad love me, and I love them. That wouldn't change. But don't I have a right to know who I am?"

Slowly Marianne lifted her head, and Ellen realized her deep eyes were wet. "Ellen, please . . ."

Something told Ellen to let her sister keep her secret, but her own desire—no, her desperate need, made her continue probing. "Soledad's a small town, and people talk. Marianne, is what they say true?"

"What do they say?" Her voice was sad, yet resigned. She looked at Ellen.

"They say she wasn't married to my father. They say

61

she was bad." She paused, only half-wanting the answer, now that it was so close. "But she wasn't, was she?"

"She was young, so very young. And someone close to her took advantage of her innocence."

"Marianne, they say something else too."

Marianne kept looking at her, waiting for the words.

"Some of them say you are my mother. Are you?" Ellen saw in Marianne's eyes the pain her words had caused. Part of her wanted to take the words back, but the need to know overcame even her love.

Finally, Marianne opened her arms uncertainly. Ellen went into them without any reservations. Their tears mingled, but they wept with relief and joy.

It was Marianne who spoke first. "I'm glad, Ellen, glad that it's finally out. Can you imagine what it's been like all these years, watching you grow up, being so very, very proud of you? We kept the secret for your sake, to keep you from being hurt."

Ellen nodded.

"We hoped there wouldn't be any gossip, Ellen, at least not by the time you were old enough to hear it."

"There wasn't much—really there wasn't." Ellen remembered Mrs. Stephens, who didn't want her son to marry a fatherless girl. But that was her burden, not Marianne's.

"I couldn't help wondering about my mother and why you were all so unwilling to talk about her, especially you, when she was supposed to be your friend. Then I heard a word here and a word there. I tried not to listen. I didn't really believe it. I thought I knew you, and you were so, well, so good, and yet . . ."

"I'm sorry, Ellen."

"For what? Surely not for being my mother."

"Never for that," Marianne told her without hesitation. "I'm sorry for disappointing you. I never wanted you to find out. I hoped this would always be my secret."

"You could have told me. So many times I asked, and so many times you lied, all of you. Why didn't you trust me with the truth?"

"It's been hard, Ellen. I guess if I'd been home all along, sometime, somehow, you would have been told. But you've been hurt just by a few words of unsubstantiated gossip. What if the whole story had gotten out? What if it does get out? You are completely blameless, but they'll blame you anyhow. The scandal . . ."

"But no one else need ever know, Marianne. Do you think I'd tell anyone? I love you. I've always loved you as my sister, and I can only love you more as my mother. Don't you know this secret is safe with me?"

"Ellen, my silence has been hard. I hated lying to you. I know it sounds crazy, but I'm not sure which I regret most—the years you didn't know or the pain knowing must be causing you. I've been so afraid you'd hate me. But you don't, do you?"

"Hate you?" Ellen hugged her close once again. "I've always loved you. I always hoped my mother was someone very much like you. You were the big sister I looked up to."

"I knew that. I revelled in it, even. One thing I don't think I could stand is your turning against me, either for having you, fatherless, or for giving you up."

Ellen studied Marianne's face. She saw sadness on it,

and fear, but mostly love. "Mother." The word did not come easily, but she was proud to say it. "Mother." It came more easily the second time. "How could I hate you for having me? And as for giving me up, did you, really?"

Ellen thought of Carrie and Matt. "I always did think it was so good of Mom and Dad to raise me after their family was practically grown," she said. "But I couldn't have dreamed all that it must have cost all three of you. Surely it would have been easier to turn me over to a stranger, or even . . ." *Girls do it all the time*, she thought, *but no, Marianne would never have considered abortion.* "Marianne, what about my father?"

But one look at Marianne's face told Ellen she must press no further. "It's all right, Mother."

Marianne put a finger to her lips. "I think I am glad you know about me, Ellen, but there are so many other people involved. Please don't ask me about your father."

"Does Paul know?"

"Yes, he does. I never could have married him with such a secret between us. The only other people who know are Mom and Dad and your Aunt Adele. And it must stay that way."

Ellen nodded. "But you were so young. It must have been very difficult for you." *That must have been when she decided to join the Salvation Army*, Ellen reflected. *Guilt? Sheer terror?*

"I wasn't alone. I never would have made it alone, but I had Mom and Dad, and the Salvation Army, and Jesus. And later, too, I had you." She sighed. "I know you have all kinds of questions, Ellen. Maybe someday I'll be able to answer them all."

Ellen took her newfound mother's hands in her own. "Someday. For now, knowing you is enough."

They finished the holiday dinner dishes. Little Pearl woke up from her nap and the three children joined them. As the sun set, Ellen put on her coat. "I've got to get back to the dorm before curfew," she explained as the youngsters protested.

"But you're coming to meeting a week from Sunday, aren't you, Aunt Ellen?" Mark asked. "We're going to sing a Chinese song, and Mommie said you'd come to hear us."

A Salvation Army Corps meeting was not Ellen's dream for a Sunday morning, but her smile was sincere. "I wouldn't miss it for the world, Mark." She hugged each of the children, then embraced Marianne. "See you Sunday, the seventh," she verified as she left.

Chapter Seven

*E*llen wished she had an excuse to skip the Sunday morning Salvation Army meeting. *I'd so much rather stay in bed. If only I hadn't promised the kids,* she muttered as she pulled a seldom-worn navy suit from her closet. *Why did I ever buy this dowdy thing?* she wondered briefly, but at least it would be more at home at the service than its wearer.

How will I act? I still can't call her "Mother." I can't treat her any differently than I always have. And do I want to? Although Ellen had suspected for years that Marianne was her mother, she still could not quite believe it. Marianne, sweet Marianne, the missionary?

Hypocrite? No. Ellen could never use that word. Whatever had happened back then, Marianne was totally sincere now. *What was she like then? A rebel, like me? A naive teenager madly in love with someone she couldn't marry? Who in the world was my father, and why didn't they just get married?*

There must have been something beyond the mere fact of the pregnancy. *Maybe not, though,* she reasoned. *In Soledad, in 1920, that would have been bad enough. After all, it's still bad enough in Soledad for Mrs. Stephens to think I'm not good enough for her son. Well, "bastard" isn't a very pretty word.* Ellen recoiled at its intrusion into her thoughts. *So what. My mother is the kindest, most decent person I know, and I'm as good as anybody.*

Perhaps Marianne's smile was more tender than usual as she greeted Ellen. Perhaps Ellen only imagined it was. She felt the tears coming to her eyes, but she blinked them back and followed her sister-mother to a half-empty row of seats near the front of the chapel.

Despite the plainness of her dress, Ellen felt out of place. Marianne's three children sang their little Chinese song, and Ellen smiled and hugged them when they returned to their seats. Then she settled down to endure the rest of the Sunday morning meeting.

It was bad enough listening to Pastor Higgins in Soledad, mouthing the same pious phrases he had been mouthing for twenty years. But the captain who was speaking today was not quoting soothing maxims; he was talking about a personal relationship with Jesus Christ, a relationship that would demand action and alter lives.

That's why Marianne lives the way she does, Ellen reflected. *That's why she's willing to work fifteen-hour days in slums while some "soldier" looks after her children. That's why she lived all those years in a hamlet in China, and why she's here now without her husband.*

Ellen wriggled on the hard folding chair. *My mother.*

Is that why? Is all this piety a sort of penance? Well, penance or not, she believes in it. And she lives it. Ellen could not admit it, even to herself, but she envied the serene woman who sat next to her.

The captain preached on, and she tried to listen. "You shall know the truth," he was quoting, "and the truth shall make you free."

How could he really think all the things scientists had discovered in the last century were lies? she asked herself. *Did he really believe all those brilliant writers and professors were instruments of the devil? Truth? Come on, now. Besides, if all that were true, God would have conquered the world by now. No good, loving, all-powerful God would endure the world as it is. He would have to heal it or destroy it.*

Ellen heard a door close at the back of the room. Heads turned. A woman slipped down the side aisle and onto the low platform. The captain stopped abruptly and turned to listen as she whispered something to him.

"My dear brothers and sisters, I have some very sad news. Sister Adams has just told me . . ." He paused, as his listeners stared at him. "The news is on the radio. The Japanese have attacked our naval base at Pearl Harbor in the Hawaiian Islands."

People turned to one another, astonished. "Japan?" "Hawaii?" "Why?"

Marianne's hand flew to her face, muffling her startled cry. "Paul."

Ellen reached out to her newfound mother. "God will protect him," she found herself saying automatically.

Chairs scraped on the floor as the congregation began to leave, but the captain called for their attention. "We all want to find radios and learn what is happening," he told them. "But first, we must pause to pray for our nation, for the young men who have been hurt, and for the families of those who have died."

The two women were silent as they ushered the children back to Marianne's apartment. "Where is Pearl Harbor, Mommie?" Mark asked. "It isn't in China, is it?"

"No, Mark, it's on an island in the Pacific Ocean in Hawaii. Don't you remember, our ship docked in Hawaii on the way from China?"

"Then it isn't where Daddy is."

The boy seemed satisfied as Marianne handed him a storybook. "Now you sit quietly and read while your sisters take their naps."

She joined Ellen in the living room. "Mark's right, of course, even though he doesn't understand," Ellen commented. "It really doesn't put Paul in any more danger than he's been in all along, does it?"

Marianne sighed, sinking onto the lumpy sofa. "At least he did have the protection of American citizenship. It didn't mean a lot, but . . ."

"But if they find him now, what happens?" Ellen asked. "He wouldn't be a prisoner of war, would he? He's a civilian."

"I don't know what his official status would be. I doubt that it matters a whole lot to the Japanese Army anyhow. If they thought he were a spy . . . That's what they usually accuse foreigners of anyhow, and if they said he was a spy . . ." Marianne shuddered. "Oh, Ellen, we must pray for him. I must trust God." She sat for several moments, head bowed, and then stood and walked to the window over-looking Chinatown's garish shop windows and signs. "Ellen, I'm being selfish, thinking only of Paul. There are so many others."

Ellen nodded. "I've been thinking about Ron. He's up in Washington state, at some air base. How long will it be before he's out there doing what they've taught him to do—killing people?" Somehow she hoped that if she did not say it, it would not happen, but the fear was too strong for silence. "And maybe getting killed."

"He expected war, Ellen. He's a brave young man, and at least he's prepared for it, if anyone can ever be prepared for war."

"He expected war with Germany. I guess we all did, though I kept hoping that somehow we'd be able to stay out of it. Hitler, well, Hitler's insane. But Japan? What have we done to them? China, yes. They're ancient enemies. But why us, why the United States?"

"Japan is a proud country with a proud history. The men who rule there believe it is Japan's destiny to rule all of Asia," Marianne explained.

"Even so, why involve the United States?"

"We've protested their actions in China."

"But surely you don't think they have a right to take over China!"

"Of course not, Ellen, but what I think isn't impor-tant. It's what the Japanese rulers think. They want China, and we've interfered by trying to cut off their supply of raw materials, like oil."

"It's not our war, Marianne." She heard a newsboy on

the crowded street below and reached for her purse. "At least it wasn't until today."

Marianne had turned on the radio when Ellen came back upstairs with the paper. Half the front page screamed one word—WAR.

They lost track of time as they listened to the terrible stories, half news, half rumor. It had been just after dawn in Hawaii. At first no one understood what was happening. Most of the American planes had been destroyed on the ground, and many American men died as they ran toward them, trying to take off and fight back. Thousands more died on ships anchored in the harbor.

Ellen tried to imagine the horror. Death falling from the air; fires raging, fed by the fuel oil in ships and planes and storage tanks.

Marianne, who had seen Chinese villages left in ruins by bombers, painted reluctant word pictures. "It's the helplessness, mostly. You can't do anything to stop it. They drop bombs. Roofs cave in. Walls burst out. Fires spring up everywhere. The noise—the explosions and the screams and the weeping."

Ellen, like Marianne, could imagine other scenes. They were nurses, and they thought of what the hospitals in Honolulu and at Pearl Harbor must be like. "The burns," Ellen said softly. "Burns are the worst."

"Yes, but the fear too. Terror is the worst thing. There is no medicine for that, and bandages don't help either. Blood—I know, you're a nursing student, and the sight of blood doesn't bother you that much, but it simply terrifies a lot of people."

Marianne bit her lip to hold back her tears as she

continued. "At least in the Chinese villages there wasn't much glass. I never thought of that as a blessing before, but people in Honolulu must have been cut to ribbons by all that flying glass from broken windows."

"They'll need a lot of blood plasma." Ellen finally shoved aside the fright and began to concentrate on the future. "We'll have to have blood drives. We'll need better ways to preserve plasma, and whole blood, too, so we can ship it."

"They'll need so many nurses." Marianne glanced toward the bedroom door.

"You can't be thinking of going to war, Marianne. The children need you." Ellen thought of her own plans. She was still over a year from her degree, a year and a half from capping. "I wish I'd skipped college now," she said, half to herself.

"So you'd have your R.N. already?" Marianne asked. "Yes, but you couldn't have known. And maybe it's selfish of me to say it, but I'm glad. Maybe this terrible thing will be over before you graduate."

"Maybe." Ellen thought about the last war. "Maybe now that we're in it we can get it over with as quickly as last time." She glanced at the newspaper that still lay in her lap. "But we seem to have lost most of our navy."

The radio droned on. They had not really been listening, but Ellen half-heard the half-told tale. "If the Japanese do invade Hawaii, if the Japanese who live there fight with them, if the Japanese among us . . ."

As she thought of Kim, and Ken, she began to pace and answer the talking box on the table. "That's absurd. I don't care what you think. The Japanese-Americans

73

who live here consider themselves Americans, just like the Germans and Italians who have been here for generations. I know they wouldn't fight against us."

Ellen still felt numb, but she had ward rounds early the next morning. At twilight that long December Sunday she hugged Marianne and caught a trolley back to the nurses' dorm.

Kim was in their room. She hadn't turned on the lights, but the radio played persistently. "God Bless America," and "America, the Beautiful," mingled with "Eternal Father Strong to Save," and "A Mighty Fortress Is Our God." Between songs, the radio commentator told of Japanese planes appearing from nowhere over the Philippines, Guam, and other places Ellen had never heard of.

Ellen pulled the light switch. Kim's face was puffy and tear-streaked. She turned away as Ellen sat on the bed and slipped an arm around her. "I'm sorry," Kim whispered. "I'm so sorry."

"But Kim, why? It's a terrible thing, but it isn't your fault."

Kim shook her head violently. "How could they do this?" She fought back sobs. "Ellen, how could my father's people do this to us all?"

"I thought maybe you could tell me," Ellen answered sadly. "Marianne and I have been asking ourselves all afternoon, why us?"

Kim shook her head. "I guess they have reasons, or excuses anyhow. This thing about the oil embargo—Papa gets letters from his brother, and the Japanese were very angry about that."

"Then you knew this might happen?" Ellen would not believe Kim could have expected this, this unspeakable outrage.

Kim fought back tears again. "Oh, no. Never this, that they would go to war, and this way, especially, with no warning, no hint even. No, Ellen, I'm as horrified as you. But, well, there was resentment, too, about the immigration laws for instance."

"Immigration laws? Why? Surely the Japanese government didn't want Japanese people to come here anyhow."

"No, I guess not." Kim studied Ellen's puzzled face. "But the insult. Surely you can see that the ban on Japanese immigration is . . ." She paused. "Well, it certainly could be considered an insult. Doesn't it really say that Americans, many Americans at least, don't think Japanese are as good as Europeans?"

Ellen recalled another law, the one against intermarriage. "I guess I never thought of it that way," she answered. "But still, that isn't everyone. And that doesn't justify . . ."

"Of course it doesn't." Kim pounded a fist into her tear-soaked pillow. "Nothing justifies what they have done, nothing. Thousands have already died; millions will die, both Japanese and Americans. Your brother, your cousins, my brother. My cousins, too, cousins I have never met. Your friend Ron, and so many like him. Oh, Ellen." She buried her face in her hands. "Oh, Ellen."

Chapter Eight

A steady splatter of late February rain blew against the window from clouds so low they shrouded the view Ellen's roommate loved so much, and might never see again. Ellen smoothed the folds of Kim's crisp uniform and laid it carefully in a suitcase. Kim, moving almost mechanically from dresser to bed and back again, had nearly filled a second, and larger, bag.

"Thanks for the help, Ellen, but I'll finish that. Ken will be picking me up pretty soon."

"I'm sorry, Kim. It's just that I can't really believe we're doing this. You're an American citizen. It isn't right. It isn't fair."

"Please, Ellen, stop it. If you say 'it isn't fair' once more, I'm going to scream."

"But . . ."

"Of course it isn't fair." For Kim, usually so soft spoken, it almost was a scream. "At first I didn't believe it. Surely they wouldn't force us to leave school. Kenji and

I are both just a few months from graduation. What harm could we do just by staying here, where we've always lived, at least until we finished school?"

"It's illegal!" fumed Ellen. "It's unconstitutional! It's imprisonment without due process of law. Whatever happened to 'innocent until proven guilty,' for crying out loud?"

"It's war," Kim said flatly.

"At least they could have given you time, let you move inland."

"At first they said we could. When Papa called and said he was trying to leave the store, that was what we expected. Papa has a cousin in Utah. He planned to go to another store there. I thought Ken and I could stay here until June, and then move. I could finish training at a hospital there, instead of here. Ken could get an internship somewhere away from the coast. But the relocation order says now, this week."

"It reminds me of the stories we hear about Germany." Ellen shuddered. "They're taking you to Tanforan—to a tent camp at a racetrack. And for no reason but that your father was born in Japan."

"Everyone is afraid, Ellen."

"Of those crazy rumors? You don't really believe Japanese have sabotaged anything here. Even in Hawaii they haven't come up with any real proof."

"People are human. It may have happened. One or two traitors, maybe. But what has the truth got to do with anything anyhow? Everyone believes it, and so they are frightened."

Kim closed the empty dresser drawer and turned to

her desk. Methodically, she began stacking textbooks in an orange crate. "We're frightened, too, you know. Maybe this is best for us. People have done things. Some Issei—the older people born in Japan—have been beaten; some of their businesses have been vandalized."

Again Ellen thought of Germany. "I always said it couldn't happen here, Kim. When the stories came out about Germany and the Jews I swore it couldn't happen here."

"And I know it won't, Ellen. It won't be like that. They'll just keep us in the transit camps for a little while. We'll find places to move where we're not so close to the coast or to the military bases. We'll be okay. You're right; this is America. There are too many decent people here, like you."

The crate was full of books. Ellen had emptied Kim's side of the closet onto her bed, and now Kim rolled the last striped apron and tucked it into the suitcase as Ken called from the foot of the stairs. "Kim, are you ready?"

As the girls lugged the heavy suitcases down the stairs, they heard Ken mumble, "I couldn't get a cab, Kim. We'll have to manage the luggage on the bus."

"I'm surprised they didn't send a truck for you," Ellen cried. "That's the way the Nazis do it."

Ellen had not seen Ken since that afternoon at the Palace. *Now it really is "good-bye,"* she realized. "Ken, you're an American citizen. So is Kim. So are most of you. Why don't you fight back?"

"And prove the government leaders are right?" There were dark circles under Ken's black eyes, and the familiar glint of humor was gone. "Oh, I've thought about it. Most of us have. A bunch of us guys were talking late last night,

79

and the night before too. Most nights, I guess, since Roosevelt signed the evacuation order."

"And you decided to just buckle under and go? Go off to who knows where, for who knows how long, in the middle of your schooling, in the middle of your life? Ken, what our government is doing to you is unconstitutional, as well as immoral. You must resist. Surely the courts will override this crazy plan."

"I think they will, eventually, but it could take years. Most of us feel we should simply do as we're told, go along with the evacuation. That is the best way to prove we are loyal Americans."

Ken sighed as he picked up the heavy suitcases. "Come on, Sis. We have to be downtown in less than an hour."

Ellen couldn't just let them walk away. She hugged Kim, her tears mingling with her friend's. Ken held a hand out, stiffly. Ellen noticed his nails, always so impeccably groomed, were now broken and rough. She took his hand in hers, and then stood on tiptoe and kissed him one last time.

It was strange having a room to herself again after two years in Berkeley and almost two in San Francisco with Kim. Ellen missed the clutter and the confidences. She missed Ken too.

"We could have faced them all down and built a good life together," she insisted to Marianne a few weeks later, as they quietly celebrated Ellen's twenty-first birthday. "Now we'll never have the chance."

"I feel sorry for your friends, Ellen. What our government is doing is unjust. But you know I never believed you and Ken had enough of a relationship to build a marriage on." She caught Ellen's eye and held it. "Maybe you thought so. Did he?"

"If you mean, did he ever propose, no," Ellen admitted. "But he thought of it. Otherwise, why would he have even mentioned that stupid law? But we could have gotten around it. We could have gone away."

"It would have been very hard. I have seen a few mixed marriages. I'm ashamed to admit it, but even in the Salvation Army it's seldom allowed."

"That doesn't sound like a very Christian attitude," Ellen protested.

"No, it isn't. And maybe someday everyone will learn that. But for now, even when both people are committed Christians and most of their friends are committed Christians, there are just too many problems."

"What if Paul were Chinese, or what if you'd fallen in love with a Chinese instead?"

Marianne thought a moment. "I was in love with Paul before I went to China, so it's hard to imagine. If he were Chinese, Ellen, I honestly don't know."

"You'd have fallen in love with him anyhow, I think. Could you have walked away from him then, without a fight?"

"It wasn't exactly love at first sight," Marianne admitted with a chuckle. "Not for me, anyhow. Paul grew on me. And no, I don't think I would have fallen in love with him, because I don't think the opportunity would have been there. We simply would never have begun seeing each other."

She cast an adoring glance at the photograph on the

mantel. "Ours was never just a marriage of convenience—obviously. I could never wish for you a happier marriage than Paul's and mine. But convenience, suitability if you will, does play a part. Paul would never have approached me, I think, if he had not seen me as a potential wife. Nor would I have encouraged his first advances if I had not thought, as well as felt, that it was right."

She seemed lost in her memories for a few minutes. "Ellen, maybe it was better then, when we took dating more seriously, when dating was really thought of as courtship. We didn't let ourselves get too close too soon. We tried to avoid temptation."

"Now you sound like Dad explaining why Christians don't dance." She started to say more, to ask if Marianne were speaking of her own temptation.

But Marianne spoke first. "And you love to dance, and you can't see that it gives you any wrong notions. Maybe not. But think about it, Ellen. Marriage is for life, and a lifetime can be very long. Doesn't the old-fashioned way make some sense?"

"Maybe we should go back to arranged marriages."

Ellen's laugh was bitter, but Marianne's was real. "Now you've got me. No, I wouldn't want that."

"Then tell me, if we should only date prospective husbands, how do we find out who the prospective husbands are? Should we limit ourselves to the kids we grew up with? You didn't."

"You do meet people, Ellen. You do get to know them, by working with them, by socializing at parties, at church. And when someone comes along who seems right, like Paul did for me, you take it one step at a time."

"And if he's the wrong color you turn your back on him. No. You know that's wrong as well as I do."

Marianne sighed. "Of course it's wrong, and I'm proud that you believe so, but we're talking about building a family. That doesn't happen in a vacuum. You cannot shut out the rest of the world, no matter what the poets say."

"Yet you agree the rest of the world is wrong. How will it ever change if some of us don't step out and show the way?"

Marianne smiled, a loving little half-smile. "Ellen, how can I argue with that kind of logic? But I love you. Pathfinders have a hard life, and we who love you don't want that for you. Ken loved you, I think. He saw into the future and he stopped dating you, too late, maybe, but he did cut it off, because he saw that you would only be hurt in the long run."

Ellen would not admit Marianne was right. "I suppose you wonder why I broke up with Ron," she snapped. His last letter sat on her dresser, another of those long, newsy letters that always seemed to end up trying to convert her. "We should have been an ideal match."

"I didn't say anything about Ron, Ellen. I gather you simply didn't love him. All the common background in the world can't make up for that."

"I thought once that I loved him, Marianne. I had a crush on him when I was only a sophomore in high school and he was a senior. I even remember Mom warning me I was too young to get serious. Then I carried the torch for him all the way through my senior year in high school, and went steady with him for almost two years at Cal."

"Why did you break up, Ellen?"

"Believe it or not, because we didn't have enough in common." Ellen laughed. "We grew up together all right, but at college we grew apart. He was all keyed up over the war; I joined the peace movement. He kept going to church, singing in the choir, and everything. Actually, it was Ron who broke it off," she admitted.

Ellen paused. The pain of losing Ken brought back the hurt of losing Ron. "Ron said he couldn't marry an unbeliever. So you see, he's just like all those Soledad people. I didn't care if he wanted to be religious, but he couldn't tolerate my open-mindedness."

Marianne pursed her lips, but kept silent.

"I know you still believe the Bible, Marianne, and I respect your beliefs, but, well, the more I learned about evolution, the laws of nature . . . Marianne, surely you know how few people believe the way you do anymore. And I just can't."

Marianne nodded. "You and a lot of other people have trouble taking God at his word, especially when it seems in conflict with our own wisdom."

Ellen started to protest. "Don't worry," Marianne told her. "I'm not going to argue Darwin, or anything else, with you. I'm just going to keep praying. One day, when you need him, you'll turn back to Jesus."

"Is that what happened to you?"

Marianne nodded. "Like you, I was raised to be God-fearing, but, yes, it was when I really needed him that God became the center of my life. I know many, many people who dedicate their lives to God without going through that kind of suffering first, but I guess some of us have thicker heads. With some of us, God has more trouble getting our attention."

"Funny, I got a letter from Ron the other day, and he said exactly the same thing. I told him I'd just as soon skip that lesson."

"Is Ron still in Washington?"

"So far. He says he's itching to get into action, but he still hasn't heard much," she answered. "He did send me a new address. Said it was just more government red tape, some number at a post office in New York. The army forwards it wherever he is, I guess."

Marianne nodded. "If he were going overseas he wouldn't be able to tell you where anyhow."

"Why, that must be it," Ellen agreed. "He must be going overseas and can't say so."

"I'm glad you're still writing to him."

"Why not, Marianne? We're old friends, and they say letters from home are good for morale."

"And letters to 'home' too," Marianne said softly.

Ellen caught the wistfulness in her voice. "How long has it been since you heard from Paul, Marianne? Has there been any word since Pearl Harbor?"

Marianne folded her hands as if in prayer, and her eyes dropped as she answered. "There was a letter smuggled out to Hong Kong in January. But now that Hong Kong has fallen, there will be no way."

"And no way for him to get out either." Ellen's hand covered Marianne's. "Marianne, I may not believe the way you do anymore, but I do still believe there has to be a God up there somewhere. And if he cares about any of us, he must be looking out for Paul. You always said you trusted the Chinese people in the villages. Won't they keep him hidden?"

"As long as the Japanese don't occupy the village, he's probably safe enough. The last I heard their army was concentrated in the major cities and along the coast. Actually, they may be less able to control China now that they are preoccupied in Indochina and the East Indies. Surely," she mused, "they don't have enough troops to fight us and the French and the British and patrol the Chinese interior too."

"I hear they might invade Australia too."

Marianne's voice was edged with fear, "Why not? They've already bombed Darwin."

"Marianne, we're going to win. You know that, don't you?"

"I have to believe so, and I do, really. The United States is bigger; we have more resources; and I know God is on our side. But we've been hurt badly. It may take years."

"Mommie," Mark called from the bedroom where the children had been playing. "Mommie, is it time for Aunt Ellen's birthday cake?"

"Just about." Marianne reached for her purse and handed the boy a quarter. "Run down to the drug store, Mark, and get us a pint of ice cream to go with it."

As Mark skipped off down the street, Marianne turned to her oldest child. "I wish it were a happier birthday, Ellen."

"It's been a very special day, Marianne."

"Because you're officially grown-up now?"

"No." She hugged Marianne warmly. "Because I'm spending it with my mother."

Chapter Nine

The war news was not good in early 1942. Most of the Pacific fleet had been destroyed or badly damaged at Pearl Harbor. Wake Island had been captured almost immediately. The British colonies of Singapore and Hong Kong had been forced to yield. The Philippines had fallen after a heroic holding action at Bataan and Corregidor.

The home front had mobilized almost overnight, outraged by the attack on Pearl Harbor and by stories of Nazi atrocities. Ellen was caught up in bond drives and blood drives. Like every other housewife, Marianne saved used cooking grease and tin cans. On the farm, Matt and Carrie planted every square yard, and in the city, Marianne's children started a Victory Garden in a planter box on the roof.

By mid-summer optimism was running high again. Americans were convinced the United States was invincible. What was left of the American navy won substantial victories in the Coral Sea and at Midway Island. From England, where Ron was stationed, American bombers had begun to carry their deadly loads into Germany itself.

A special piece of good news came in July for Marianne, and she rushed to share it with Ellen. "A man who flew on the Doolittle raid brought it," she explained, as she showed her daughter the wrinkled scrap of paper. "He was in our village . . . He saw Paul . . . He brought me a letter from Paul!"

"But how?"

"After they bombed Japan, the American pilots did not have enough fuel to get back to their aircraft carrier, so they flew on to China. Most of them managed to find friendly Chinese who smuggled them across the country to Chiang Kai-shek's headquarters in Chungking. From there the Flying Tigers got them over the Hump to India."

Ellen nodded. "Yes, wasn't it wonderful the way the pilots pulled it off? But they didn't really run into Paul, did they?"

"Yes. Can you believe he actually hid one crew member in our old dispensary for a few days? And Paul's all right. The Japanese have scarcely been there at all, and the villagers have sworn secrecy. He's safe, Ellen. Thank God he's safe."

The letter from Paul was written in agonizingly tiny script on a blank half-page torn from a medical text. Marianne seemed unable to let go of it, but read parts aloud:

Our friends and our God have been with me. I have very little medicine, but I can do something, sometimes, to ease the suffering. And in the midst of the war, the gospel brings its

*own peace. There is a risk in sending this note. If the lieuten-
ant should be caught and tortured, the Japanese might kill
those who have hidden me. But I must let you know I am
alive, at least, and that I love you. Pray for us all.*

Ellen's letters from Ron arrived more regularly. They
came on thin blue sheets designed to save space and
weight. They soaked up ink like a blotter. And sometimes,
if Ron had been careless with sensitive information, words
or phrases would be cut out by the censor, leaving behind
a flimsy pale blue paper doily.

Ron's letters were brotherly—warm and gossipy. "The
fellows tease me when I tell them you aren't 'my girl,'" he
had written once. "But your letters mean so much to me.
Mom's do, too, of course, but she writes about the family,
and the Valley. I depend on you to keep me up to date on
the rest of the home front."

So she kept writing to Ron, as she did to her cousins.
She told them about the latest blood drive she had helped
with, and the hundred units of plasma her group had
collected. "We're all behind you now," she assured Ron.
"You were right all along. War is the only language Hitler,
Tojo, and their ilk understand."

She told him about the children who died or who were
crippled by the infantile paralysis epidemic that summer.
She asked why his God created such a terrible disease, and
she was not surprised when he had no answer.

Ellen told him about her rage at the internment of the
Nisei, and at the people who could not separate them
from the evil Japanese government; and she was just a
little surprised when he shared her anger.

She told him Marianne had heard from Paul, skipping the details that might, somehow, endanger Paul and the friendly Chinese. She even considered telling him the other news about Marianne, that the woman she had always thought of as her older sister was really her mother. *Why?* she wondered. *Why should I share something that personal with someone who is just an old friend?* Instead, she filled the pages with good-natured grumbling about bittersweet chocolate and baggy rayon stockings.

Kim wrote to Ellen from a place called Manzanar. "It's pretty awful," Kim conceded, "but we try to make the best of it. The wind, oh, that incessant wind, and the dust. But then, why should a little wind and dust bother someone from King City?" she rationalized.

Ellen scarcely knew how to write to her old friend. Surely the news about school, about classmates' engagements, about her own plans to join the Army Nurse Corps would only make Kim feel more isolated.

Ellen did write about the Fair Play Committee that some of their old friends at Berkeley had formed to protest the internment, and Kim thanked her for that. "Your letters remind me that we do still have friends out there. Sometimes I almost forget there is an 'out there,'" she wrote, with a rare admission of bitterness.

"We're okay," she assured Ellen. "We have enough to eat and a roof over our heads, even though we are pretty crowded. But it's so good to know we aren't forgotten. And it's such a waste. We should be out there helping this country, our country, to win this war. Most of us are as angry as you are about what the Japanese government has done to America. But we try to understand. We're different, and they just can't trust us *because* we're different."

Kim scarcely mentioned Ken, and when the letter came from him just before Thanksgiving, Ellen realized that she had almost forgotten how much she had missed him at first. *Why is he writing? Has something happened to Kim?* she wondered.

"Kim said she'd let you know, Ellen," he wrote, "but I wanted to tell you myself. I have good news—two pieces of good news, in fact. First, I have been given permission to leave camp to continue my education. The University of Michigan Medical School in Ann Arbor has accepted me for the spring semester, and I will be leaving in a few weeks. So I've only lost a year, really."

Oh, I'm so glad, she thought. *It must have been so frustrating for him working as an orderly in the camp infirmary when he was less than a semester from his M.D.*

She read on. "And, Ellen, before I leave I am getting married. Midori has permission to go with me. She's a nurse, like you, and the hospital there has offered her a job."

If she felt anything, Ellen realized, it was a tiny pang of bitterness that he had turned back so easily to his first love.

"Midori is a lovely girl," Ken continued. "Surprisingly, our parents have had this planned since we were children. We dated when we were in high school, because everyone expected it. But, being liberated American kids, once we got away from home we ignored each other. Suddenly, here, we found ourselves drawn together again. It is good, Ellen. It is right. Please be happy for us."

"And I am," she told Marianne over their Thanksgiving dinner together. "Funny, isn't it? A year ago I was so depressed because he'd broken off with me. I did care for him, Marianne. I still do. But you were right. It wasn't love, not the kind of love a marriage is built on."

"It's been quite a year, hasn't it?" Marianne mused aloud. "A year ago today . . ." She glanced at her three young children engrossed in their turkey and sweet potatoes, and didn't finish.

A year ago today you told me you were really my mother, Ellen remembered. *The only other thing on my mind then, other than Ken, was wondering how I could get you to tell me about my father. Someday maybe. . .* "Only a year," she murmured.

"We're thankful Mommie got a letter from Daddy," Mark interjected. "And we're thankful none of our cousins have gotten killed in the war yet, and we pray for them every day."

"The war," Ellen sighed. "A year ago I still hoped we wouldn't be drawn into this war. I still thought there was a chance we could keep out of it. Now I'm chafing at the bit. I can't wait to graduate and start doing my part."

"You still plan to enlist, then?"

"I don't feel as if I have a choice, Marianne. My friends and cousins are overseas risking their lives defending me. And there is a desperate shortage of nurses. Next July seems such a long way off, but I do have to finish my class work so that I can get my degree in January."

"Then you still have six months of supervised ward

work before you're capped. Do you think that will be at the University Hospital?"

"I don't know. I used to hope so, and up until the war most of the graduates were assigned there. But now they are sending us all over the city. Even Letterman Army Hospital is taking a few, and Fort Miley Veterans' Hospital. The training might be better at the university, but if I'm going to be an army nurse anyhow, I might as well get started."

Just after Christmas another letter came from Ron. She tore it open eagerly. He was still in England. She had heard the news on the radio about the daylight bombing raids the small American Army Air Corps was making into Germany and she guessed he was part of it. *It must be terribly dangerous*, she thought.

But Ron didn't talk about the raids much. "Sometimes we can't go out for days at a time because of bad weather," he told her. "The Flying Fortress is a great plane. Our crew is top notch, and the Lord's up there with us."

This time he wrote about Christmas:

It could have been really rough, but these Brits are swell to us G.I.'s, Ellen. I went to a couple of dances, but I guess I'm still an old-line Methodist. Besides, some of the fellows get to drinking, being so lonesome and all, and well, you know I don't feel comfortable with that.

Ever the good Christian. Ellen let herself smile. *You'd think he'd take every chance he could to have some fun. But then,* she reflected, *he needs that faith. How can they stand it, the ones who don't trust some higher power?*

She read on:

For Christmas one of the churches in a nearby town organized a "Home for Christmas" party. They had a tree and carols, and then each family invited two or three of us for dinner. Of course they don't have a lot to share with us, but the spirit is what counts. I took them a fruitcake my mother had sent. It was hard as a rock, but it sure went over big. The English really like their sweets, and sugar is strictly rationed.

Here too, she thought. *It's probably a blessing in disguise, for our teeth anyhow.*

The family that entertained my buddy and me was very nice. Mr. Blanchard is a plumber—talked a lot about patching pipes and how hard it was to get parts. They have a son in North Africa with Montgomery, and a daughter. Believe it or not her name is Ellen, too, and she's an army nurse at a base not far from here. We hit it off pretty well. She invited me to a party the YMCA's having at her base on New Years' Eve, and I'm looking forward to it.

I wonder if she's pretty. Ellen reread the last paragraph. *So what if she is,* she told herself. *But she's English. If having things in common is so important, doesn't that count?* She folded the letter and tucked it into her dresser drawer with the others. *After all, it's none of my business. I should be glad he's found someone to have a good time with.*

Chapter Ten

*E*llen received her bachelor's degree in January of 1943 and was assigned to Fort Miley Veterans' Hospital for six months of supervised ward nursing. Fort Miley would not have been her first choice, she confessed to one of the older nurses during a lunch break. "It's depressing. So many of the patients here are old, chronically ill, dying. There's so little we can do for them."

May, the older woman, sighed. "I know what you mean. I worked in pediatrics when I was young, but I knew going back to work at my age would be hard. When the war started I wanted to do my duty, and I thought it would be easier here. It is, in a way."

"Custodial care!" Ellen grumbled. "We're nurses. We're trained for more important things than treating bedsores and doling out pain killers."

"More important?"

"Saving lives, not just easing dying. Anybody can do that."

"Maybe it doesn't take a college degree. I hope not, because I don't have one. But these men gave their all, like my sons are doing now, and I'm not ashamed of comforting them, even when comfort is all I can give."

"I'm not ashamed of it," Ellen defended. "It's important, and you're doing a wonderful job. But . . ." *Why did I have to add that "but"?* Ellen thought. *Am I really so conceited as to think this work is beneath me?* "I'm sorry, May. That sounded terrible. Of course these veterans deserve the best we have to give them."

"Good, because I was thinking of asking a favor of you, Ellen."

"Of me? Sure. What?"

"There's a man in one of the wards who's from your hometown. He says he has no family. He's dying, slowly, but surely. And he seems so lonely. I hoped you'd visit him. Maybe you'd know someone down there who might remember him, though I gather he's been away from Soledad for a long time."

"From Soledad? My family's lived there for over forty years. If he lived there long enough to think of it as home, I'm sure my Mom and Dad or one of my uncles at least would have known him."

"You'll go see him then?" May asked eagerly. "He was gassed back in the First World War, and now he's in the TB ward. His name is Arnesen—mean anything to you?"

Ellen frowned thoughtfully. "Arnesen? It sounds familiar. I don't think there's anybody in Soledad by that name now. But I'm sure I've heard it before."

"I'll tell him you'll be up. I think a pretty face with

news from home will cheer him up. That's Arnesen, Eric Arnesen."

Ellen gasped, "Eric! Of course. Eric Arnesen."

"You do know of him, then."

"I didn't recognize the name at first. He left the Valley before I was born," Ellen explained, "and no one ever uses the name anymore, but my Grandmother McLean's first husband was named Arnesen. They had a son . . ."

"Eric! Oh, Ellen, how wonderful. If he could only be reconciled to his family before it's too late. Is his mother still alive?"

"Gran's in her seventies, and she's frail. But I know she still grieves for Eric. I think seeing him again would make her happier than anything else."

"Even if he's dying, Ellen?"

"I never knew just what happened, May. I've heard he was gassed, and came home from the war a semi-invalid. Then a girl he'd been going with married my Uncle Tim—that's his stepbrother. They say Eric disappeared the night of the wedding, and no one in Soledad has heard from him since. I know Gran would want to see him." She paused to ponder. "Yes, even if it meant losing him all over again."

"I'm sure seeing her would comfort him. He does talk some about his mother. He seems to think he hurt her, and it bothers him. If she has forgiven him for whatever happened, it would mean a lot to him to know it."

"If I'm right, and this is Gran's son, I can't imagine what there would be to forgive. She's never spoken of him with anything but love, May. I'll talk to him before I write to anyone at home, but if I believed in miracles I guess I'd think this was one."

The TB ward was the gloomiest part of the gloomy veterans' hospital. Ellen's heart sank as she entered it garbed in the hospital's regulation isolation gown, cap, and mask. The men in the ward ranged from downy-cheeked kids just back from the South Pacific to wrinkled veterans of the Spanish-American War.

She went to Eric's bedside almost by instinct. Though his ashen face bore no resemblance to Anna McLean's, there was something about the wide blue eyes and the gray-streaked golden hair that drew her to him.

"Hello, there," she said with forced cheer. "May told me about you. She said you're from my hometown."

"Oh," he muttered, turning his head away from her. "Which one?"

Somehow she'd pictured a tearful, joyful reconciliation. But his cold response warned her to go slowly. "May said you were from Soledad. I grew up near there."

"I've been away for years—since before your time."

She forced a friendly laugh, though the harshness in his voice frightened her. *The least I can do is be nice to him,* she thought. *Maybe if I take it easy I can break through this shell he's built up.* "But it's a small town. Do you have any family there?"

"I don't have any family." He still kept his face turned away from her. "Not there, or anywhere else."

"That must be awful," she said. "I have a wonderful family—not just my mother and dad, but sisters, a brother, a whole flock of aunts and uncles, and a marvelous grandmother too. Did you have a family when you were in Soledad?" she prodded gently.

"It was a long time ago, I told you." He coughed. "Twenty years. Closer to twenty-five, I guess."

"I guess you did leave before I was born then." She moved around the bed. "I'm tired of talking to the back of your head," she teased with the soft chuckle she had inherited from her mother.

He looked at her then and seemed puzzled. *He couldn't know me*, she told herself. *He left before I was born, and I don't look anything like my mother or any of the Hanlons.*

He stared at Ellen for a few seconds, and then turned away again. "Look, I'm sure you're a nice kid, and you mean well, but May's got it all wrong. She figures I shouldn't die alone."

"Nonsense," Ellen lied. "You're not going to die."

"Have it your way."

"I usually do." She laughed again. "I don't give up easily, and neither does May."

"Listen, kid, I've been a loner for a long time. Nobody owes me anything."

"Mr. Arnesen, everyone needs someone. It's no crime."

"Nurse Whoever-you-are—" He coughed again. "I have no family, and I don't deserve to have a family. Forget it. Just leave me alone."

He struggled to sit up, gasping for air, and Ellen poured water from the bottle beside his bed and held the cup to his lips. His breathing eased. She fluffed the pillows as he leaned back into them. "All right. You just rest for now.

By the way, my name's Ellen, and I'm coming back and visit later."

He shook his head in a feeble no.

"Just to visit," she assured him. "If you don't want to talk about your family or Soledad, we'll talk about something else."

She did visit him, almost daily, and he seemed to enjoy her visits as long as she did not mention Soledad or question him about his family.

"I brought some magazines," she told him brightly one warm spring evening. She laid copies of *Look* and *The Saturday Evening Post* on the bed.

A semblance of a grin appeared as Eric looked at the Rockwell cover on the *Post*. "Baseball season again. I used to be quite a ballplayer in my younger days, back before the War—the first one, that is."

"Pitcher?" she asked, grateful for a neutral subject.

"No, shortstop." He almost laughed, though the effort forced a hacking cough. "Not a bad hitter, though. I was little, but I had a good eye for a pitch, and I was fast."

Ellen smiled, then, at an off-hand remembrance. "My uncles used to play a lot of baseball in Soledad. They've mentioned a little guy they knew once, who packed a terrific wallop with a baseball bat."

"Yeah? Well I didn't play much there. If you just came back to pry, you can get out right now."

She groped for another, safer, topic. "Do you think the Yankees will win the pennant again this year, Mr. Arnesen?"

"Please call me Eric, Ellen. Mr. Arnesen was my father."

Ellen smiled at the older man.

"And don't bet on the Yankees without DiMaggio," he warned. "Personally I'd like to see the Tigers do it again."

"They've got the pitching, but somebody has to hit. Why Detroit?" she asked. "Any particular reason?"

He shrugged. "Lived there for a while back when Cobb was still managing, and then they had Mickey Cochrane, Charlie Gehringer. Now there's a ballplayer's ballplayer. And Greenberg. Even way out here people admit Hank Greenberg's a whale of a threat at the plate."

Eric had to fight for a long breath. "Of course Hank's off to war now too. But there's something about Detroit—it's a great sports town. Once a Tiger fan, always a Tiger fan, I guess."

"So you lived in Detroit a long time then?"

"As long as I lived any one place. Had my life pretty well together there. Even thought I might get married and settle down."

"Are you sorry you didn't?"

He put a finger to his lips in gentle, teasing reproof. "And how come a pretty thing like you is still single? Do you have a beau off in the army, maybe?"

"Not really."

"You sound sad. Want to talk about it? It would be safer than talking about me," he added.

She smiled. "You're right. Sometimes it helps to talk things out with a stranger." *Besides, the best way to get him to open up may be to involve him in my life*, she reasoned. "I guess I haven't met the right fellow yet," she told him truthfully. "I went with a Soledad boy for quite a while. We went to high school and college together, but, well, we disagreed about some things that were pretty important—to him at least."

"So he broke it off. I can understand how you feel."

"Well, he didn't exactly break it off. We just decided, both of us, that it couldn't come to anything. He's in England now, in the Air Corps. We're still friends, but we both agreed we had no future together. He's seeing someone, an English girl."

"You say you're just friends, but I can tell you're hurt. I had a girl once . . ."

"In Detroit?"

"There, too, but I was remembering the one in Soledad. I went to war and she married someone else."

"I'm sorry," she said gently. "It wasn't like that with Ron and me. I don't think we ever were really in love—just kids in love with the idea of being in love. No, I'm glad he's found someone else."

"But you're sorry you haven't."

"I guess so." She thought of Ken and sighed. "I thought I had, but now he's gone too."

"Not twice rejected? Not anyone as sweet as you. Another soldier?"

"No, not a soldier. They won't let him fight. He's Japanese."

Eric frowned. "You're in love with a Jap?"

"He's Nisei, Japanese-American. Eric, he's as good an American as anyone."

"You're lucky to be rid of him."

She shook her head. "No. It wouldn't have been easy for us, but we could have made it work. But they shipped him off to a relocation camp," She stopped, unwilling to tell Eric she'd been rejected twice.

Eric looked directly at her then, as he seldom did. "Ellen, don't let it make you bitter. Don't ever let it make you hurt yourself, or anyone else." His eyes watered. "Especially someone else."

Ellen kept visiting Eric, and not just for his sake. He was easy to talk to as long as she avoided Soledad and questions about his family. She brought him a little table radio. "You can at least get the Tigers' scores," she told him with the little unconscious laugh that she never quite connected with the shadow that so frequently crossed his face. "I'll have to turn you into a San Francisco Seals fan."

His own refusal to discuss his past seemed, perversely, to force her to talk about hers. "But Ron was always so religious," she explained. "I guess I did turn to Kenji somewhat on the rebound."

"Hard to figure a pretty girl like you getting involved with someone like that, but I suppose there are some nice Japs too," he conceded.

"Awfully nice, Eric." He seemed to be in an unusually agreeable mood, so she decided to try her luck again. "You know, my folks have lived around Soledad for two generations, but I don't know any Arnesens." *I'm not lying*, she told herself. *I don't know any except him.*

"Pa died years ago. I went away, probably before you were born. And I told you there's nothing there I care anything about, nothing at all."

"What about your mother?" she asked softly, remembering the wistful tone of Gran's voice whenever she mentioned her firstborn son.

"My mother was a saint." He stared at Ellen, the puzzled frown coming back once more. "My mother was a saint, and I broke her heart."

"Are you sure? Mothers' hearts don't break easily."

"You haven't any idea what happened, Ellen. And you can quit trying to find out right now. I've carried my guilt for half my life, and I can carry it a little while longer. It's the least I can do."

"You said your mother was a saint. Maybe she still is, and if she is, she would forgive you anything. Maybe the one thing she wants is to see you again."

His eyes searched hers. She was afraid her probing had gone too deep. "Ellen, I can't put my finger on it, but I know you're not being honest with me. Anyhow, there are a lot of rocks in this world that are better not turned over. Whatever you know, or think you know, forget it."

"You're right," she confessed, almost without thinking. "I know your mother. And I know she loves you, Eric. Please let me write and tell her you're here."

"No!" He shouted the word, and it seemed to Ellen that it took every ounce of strength left in his frail body. "No. Please, please, promise me you won't do that." He sank deep into the pillow, gasping. "Don't, please. You don't know."

He grasped her hand and wouldn't let go. "Promise." He struggled for air, and Ellen was terrified that he could lose his fight within minutes.

He mustn't die now, without Gran knowing. "I promise," she assured him.

It was a promise she didn't intend to keep. Yet she knew that as soon as she sent the letter home Gran would appear in San Francisco and demand to see him. And if Eric refused? What if he refused to see her? *I'll talk it over with Marianne,* Ellen decided. *She might know what happened. Maybe she'll have the answer.*

Chapter Eleven

I have to be away so much that I hate to steal any time from the children when I am home," Marianne explained to Ellen when she had, at last, put them to bed. "I'm sorry it's so late, but now we can talk, woman to woman. What's the problem?"

"Well, there is something I'd like your advice about," Ellen admitted. "I have to decide what to do soon, but it's kind of complicated."

"Are you having second thoughts about enlisting? There's plenty of worthwhile work here, if you are."

"Oh, no. I'm going to enlist. I can't wait to get over there and help our boys," Ellen insisted. "No, it isn't about me at all. It's something that concerns the family—something I've found out."

"Not bad news, I hope."

"No, good news. At least it should be good news."

"Then why are you so sober?" Marianne asked.

"I've met someone at the hospital, one of the veterans." Ellen saw Marianne's knowing smile. "No," she went on, "it's nothing like that. He's old enough to be my father, and he's very ill with TB, almost certainly dying."

"It's always hard losing a patient," Marianne sympathized, "but what has that got to do with the family?"

"He's Gran's son, Marianne—Eric, the one who went away years ago and has never been heard from since."

The color drained from Marianne's face as she muffled her gasp.

"Yes," Ellen continued, "it's quite a shock, isn't it?"

"Have you let them know at home? Does Gran know yet?"

"I haven't done anything," Ellen told her. "He's so sick I wondered if maybe it wouldn't be better for Gran not to know than to find him and then lose him all over again."

"Ellen, she has to know." Marianne seemed to be over her original shock. "After all these years of not knowing if he were alive or dead. No, she has a right to know, and to see him again."

"There's something else, Marianne. He won't talk about them at all. At first he even insisted that he didn't have a family. He won't listen to any news about them, or even about Soledad." She sighed. "I've been visiting him for several weeks, but he seemed so bitter I didn't even tell him my last name."

"I think that was wise." The words were calm, but Marianne's voice trembled. "You said he was very ill, dying. How much time is there?"

"Not much. Weeks, maybe days. I've been taking it slowly, but there's so little time left. I told him yesterday that I knew his mother, and that I knew she loved him and longed to see him again."

"Was he glad to hear that, Ellen?"

"He was appalled. When he finally realized I knew who he was he made me promise I wouldn't tell Gran. But I can't keep that promise, can I?"

Marianne sat for a long time staring at the budding geranium in the box outside her window.

"I do have to tell her, don't I? But if I do and she comes up here and he refuses to see her, wouldn't that be worse yet?"

Marianne still didn't speak.

"I told him Gran loved him. Maybe he'd believe me if he understood why I know that. Maybe if I told him who I am . . ."

Marianne jumped. "Tell him who you are?"

"Why, yes, my name. I'm his niece, sort of at least. If he knew I was family, maybe he could believe me when I tell him how much his family cares about him."

The panic Ellen thought she had seen on Marianne's face faded. "Do you know why he left Soledad, Marianne? What happened between him and Gran to cause him so much guilt?"

Marianne was silent again.

"Whatever it was," Ellen continued, "I know Gran still loves him. She doesn't talk about him much, of course, after all these years. But I never heard her say anything but good about him. So why did he go away like that?"

"Eric was sick even then," Marianne explained. "You know he was gassed in the last war. When he came home, he was very weak. He couldn't do as much as he thought he should around the farm. And he was in a lot of pain. He was taking morphine, and he started to drink."

"Wasn't there something about Uncle Tim and Aunt Nancy too?"

Marianne nodded. "Eric dated Nancy for a while before he went to France. Nobody thought it was anything serious at the time, I guess, and after he left, Tim started seeing her. One thing led to another, and by the time Tim left for France, he and Nancy were engaged. Eric took it pretty hard."

"So hard that he left town on their wedding night and never came back? That just doesn't make sense. A man might leave home because he was jilted, but he wouldn't deny his whole family, refuse to contact his own mother for nearly twenty-five years. Eric isn't eaten up by anything that was done to him. He's blaming himself for some terrible thing that, as near as I can figure out, never happened."

"We can't, any of us, know what goes on in another person's heart. Eric had done something . . ." Marianne paused abruptly, and then continued. "Eric thought he'd done something that would hurt Gran very much."

"But what? Being sick is nothing to feel guilty about."

"Leave it alone." Marianne's voice was growing surprisingly sharp. "Ellen, you're right in being kind to him, and I think you're right in wanting Gran to know he's here. She loves him, and she doesn't blame him for anything he did. But don't pry into the past. Leave it alone."

"Will you go see him, Marianne? Maybe you could convince him Gran would want to see him again."

Marianne's hands folded and unfolded. Her head bowed as if in prayer. Her eyes closed, opened, closed again, and Ellen realized there were tears in them.

She knows much more than she's telling me, Ellen realized. *Much more than she can tell me, at least right now.* As she saw the pain on the face of her sister-mother, her thoughts half-formed and reformed. *Eric disappeared before I was born, in June. In June of 1919,* she suddenly realized. *And I was born the following March.* She remembered how strangers often commented on her resemblance to her grandmother. *Oh, no. It couldn't be. It just couldn't be.*

She tried to brush away what she somehow knew was true. She fumbled for Marianne's hand. *It wasn't Aunt Nancy he loved,* she thought. *But why was that so terrible? It isn't as if he and Marianne were really related or anything. Of course she was awfully young, but . . .*

At last Marianne spoke. "Yes, I will go and see him. I must. He must not die without knowing that he has been long since forgiven for any hurt he caused. He must know they still love him."

They? It wasn't the word Ellen had expected, but she knew she mustn't press her mother any further, *not now.*

Ellen passed the door to the TB ward. She had not been in to see Eric in a week. *He was opening up to me, becoming my friend,* she reminded herself. *Does he think I found out what he did, and hate him for it? Or is he afraid I'll tell Gran in spite of my promise, or maybe that I won't?*

She had to go in. Deny it though he would, Eric needed someone. He knew her, had begun to trust her. Marianne had said she would come, *but when?* Ellen knew her mother was praying for the strength to face him. *Why should it be so hard for her, though, if she had loved him once? Does she still care? She seems so deeply in love with Paul. Is Paul the problem?*

Marianne talked about forgiving him. What had he done but love her? And abandon her, of course. The man Ellen was coming to love was not cruel, and she could not believe he had ever been cruel. *But it was a coward's way out, at best,* she knew, and her growing love was touched with bitterness. *He had abandoned her.*

I wish I believed in prayer, Ellen thought, as she dressed in the ugly isolation garb. *I can't ignore him when he needs me so much, but it's been hard enough just pretending I didn't know him. Now, how can I face him knowing he's my father and that he ran away?*

Ellen forced a casual smile as she walked to his bedside and was surprised to see his smile in response. "I'm sorry I haven't been in to see you," she said sincerely. "I've been pretty busy."

"I thought you'd given up on me, Ellen. I wouldn't have blamed you, after the way I acted."

"You felt I had no right to pry like that. Maybe I didn't."

"You meant well." The smile disappeared. "You will keep your promise, though."

"Eric," she sighed. "I think I owe you an explanation."

"Your promise," he pleaded.

"First, the explanation," she insisted. "You see, I've known who you were right from the beginning. And I do know your mother wants very much to see you."

"You told her! You meddling, no good . . ."

The words hurt more than a slap in the face. "I didn't. I still haven't."

He tried to draw a deep breath and failed. "I'm sorry. I should have trusted you."

"Why should you? I haven't been that honest with you, either. My full name is Ellen Hanlon. Your mother is my grandmother." Ellen smiled to herself, realizing for the first time how true the statement was. "So I really do know how happy it would make her to see you again."

"In spite of everything? I wish I could believe you."

"Maybe you won't believe this, Eric, but no one in Soledad, none of the McLeans or the Hanlons, know why you left." *Well, almost none,* she thought.

"Maybe you don't know." He paused, and studied her face. "Ellen Hanlon? I can't place you."

"Matt and Carrie's youngest," she explained. "You left before I was born."

"I see. Well, I can understand their not telling you about it, but . . ."

How could she tell him Gran didn't know, without telling him what she, herself, did know? Ellen studied Eric's face. The tell-tale flush of fever flared on the ashen cheeks. There was so little time. "Eric, Gran isn't well. And it would make her so happy."

"You aren't lying? You wouldn't lie? Are you sure they don't know?"

"They don't know." He seemed so very frail lying there, colorless but for the fever. Suddenly she feared Marianne's promised visit might be too much for him to bear. And yet . . .

He lay motionless for a long time, his skin gray against

the yellowing hospital linen. Almost certainly, Ellen realized, he was thinking about the one person who had to know. *How can I prepare him for seeing Marianne? How can I tell him she doesn't hate him? How do I know she doesn't, except that Marianne's incapable, I think, of hating anyone.*

At last Eric spoke, carefully phrasing the question he dare not ask. "How are they all doing? Will's a rich farmer by now, I'll bet. And Tim?" He smiled, wanly. "I was so sore at Tim for stealing my girl, but she wasn't my girl, really. We'd never talked marriage. I had thought about it, but, well, it didn't seem right to tie Nancy down with the war coming and all. Can't blame Tim for stepping in, can I?"

Did he want to ask about Marianne? She, too, evaded that subject. "My dad—Matt—and Uncle Will, and Uncle Harry have incorporated the farms—nearly a thousand acres now."

"A thousand acres!"

"You should claim your inheritance."

"Not mine. I have nothing left there," he insisted. "But I'm glad they've done well. You said Will and Harry? What about Tim?"

"Tim took over the Johnson dairy after he and Nancy were married," Ellen explained. "And he's the rich one, actually. He and Nancy built a new house a couple of years ago, very modern and stylish. Let's see, Aunt Adele's married to the principal of Salinas High School and has two kids. So Dad's the general manager of the farms. Will is business manager, and Harry's the field boss. He's always experimenting with new varieties and new sprinkler systems and new fertilizers."

Make it casual, she told herself. *Make her just one of the family litany.* "Marianne's here in San Francisco."

"Marianne." His eyes gave nothing away. "She always wanted to be a nurse."

"She is. She's married." *He looks more relieved than jealous,* Ellen thought. "Would you believe she joined the Salvation Army? She and her husband, Paul, were missionaries for several years, in China. Paul is still there, but she brought their youngsters home just before Pearl Harbor."

"That's tough. Marianne was a nice kid."

How can he look so impassive? But the nurse in her saw the pain in Eric's eyes. "She's heard from Paul a couple of times. Amazingly enough, some of the Doolittle raiders ran into him in China, so she knows he was all right up to then, at least." Ellen forced herself to keep rattling on. "And if there is a God up there who can do anything for anybody, he certainly should be looking out for Paul."

"What do you mean, 'if'?" Eric demanded. "The family was always religious. It got us through a lot. That's where I went wrong, losing my faith. You have to keep believing."

"Gran's been praying for twenty-three years for your return, Eric." Ellen could see that he was very tired, and she grasped the opportunity to steer the conversation back to the reconciliation she wanted so much for him. "But the answer to that prayer is in your hands, not God's."

He didn't answer.

"Let me phone and tell her I've found you."

115

"You said no one knew why I left," he pleaded. "But someone does. One person, at least."

She had no response.

"I can't face . . . I can't face them. If there were only some way to see Ma, alone." She could hardly hear his breathless whisper. "Ellen, please come back tomorrow."

"Can I call Gran, Eric?"

He shook his head feebly. "Not yet. Come back later."

Ellen was not sure there would be a tomorrow for him. She ached to take him in her arms and tell him she was his daughter before it was too late. But, no. Marianne would have to tell him that.

Ellen telephoned Marianne and told her Eric was nearly ready to see Anna. "He asked about you," she said.

"He did?" Marianne sounded surprised.

"Well, he asked about everyone, but he was obviously interested in you. He seemed pleased you were married and had children. He said he was sure God was watching over your husband."

"You didn't say anything about my going to see him, did you?"

"No. I thought about it, but I just didn't know what to say."

"Good."

"Marianne, I think he's ready to see Gran, but he admitted there was someone he couldn't face." She dared not add the question, *You?*

"I know you can't understand, Ellen, and I can't make you understand, certainly not over the telephone. But I have to go to him, to assure him of my forgiveness. I have to tell him that God will forgive him and that he must

116

forgive himself. And I can't do that unless I tell him, first, that I have forgiven him."

Ellen couldn't ask her questions from a public phone booth. *Forgiveness? For the act? For me! It wasn't just young love*, she concluded. *He'd run away to avoid blame. Or was the running away itself the wrong that must be forgiven?* Marianne was still talking about forgiveness, but then, she had been fifteen years old, a child herself, disgraced and deserted.

"I'll go tomorrow," Ellen heard her say firmly. "Will you meet me after your shift? I'll tell you all about it then."

"I . . . Should I go with you?"

"I don't think so, Ellen. I'm not sure, yet, how much I will tell him, even. No, I'll see him first, and then meet you."

Chapter Twelve

*F*ort Miley Veterans' Hospital stood out on the tip of the San Francisco Peninsula. A few blocks south, Golden Gate Park began its green swath through the city. To the west, the Pacific stretched all the way to China; to the north, to Alaska. Normally, in summer, a chill breeze blew misty fog across this area, but tonight, in the midst of a rare June heat wave, there was little breeze and no mist.

The weather was too nice to waste waiting inside, so Ellen sat on a bench near the hospital entrance watching Marianne's children playing on the lawn. Their mother was upstairs with Eric, and Ellen tried not to imagine what was happening. It seemed, sometimes, that the more she learned about her birth, the deeper the mystery became. When she had first begun to suspect Marianne was her mother, she had painted a picture in her mind of young love and gay abandon. Against God's law, no doubt, but at least it was romantic.

Even knowing that her father was her mother's step-uncle didn't change that picture. Eric and Marianne weren't related just because his mother happened to be her grandfather's second wife. So why hadn't he and Marianne married?

No, it was not just young love. Marianne's every look and action the past few days had made that all too clear. She said she had forgiven him. Ellen shivered. The more she thought about it the worse it became. Marianne had not gone to him willingly, had she? *And she was only fifteen. At the very least he took advantage of her ignorance.*

While a part of Ellen still longed to go to this man she had come to care for deeply and to tell him she loved him and was happy to call him "Father," much of Ellen's nature recoiled. What he had done to Marianne, to her mother, was unthinkable, but Ellen could not help thinking about it. Words, terrible words, cut into her tender heart: *Rape. Violation. Disgrace.*

Still, Marianne had forgiven him, had gone to him to tell him he was forgiven. *How long did it take for her to forgive him?* Ellen wondered. *He's dying. I need time, and I haven't got time. If I can't bring myself to go to him now, within a matter of days, I'll never have another chance.*

"Mommie's coming," Mark called.

Ellen tried to shake off the bitterness that was growing within her. "How did it go?"

Marianne glanced at the children, who clustered around them. They crossed the street in silence, and Ellen paused at the bus stop. "Why don't you walk me partway home, through the park?" Marianne suggested. "It's such a warm evening, and we can talk while the kids play."

Marianne couldn't be hurried, Ellen realized. They strolled the park's pathways, keeping pace with the little girls' short legs, until they reached the shore of Stowe Lake. Marianne reached into her purse and handed her son a few pennies. "Go buy a bag of peanuts, Mark, and you and your sisters can feed the ducks."

The children scampered off, delighted at the rare treat. Marianne sighed as she sat on a lone bench and patted the seat next to her.

Ellen joined her. "Were you able to give him any peace, Marianne?"

"I think so." She glanced at her three youngest, laughing as the ducks dove for the peanuts. "It was hard, but with God's help I think I did get through to him. He prayed with me for God's forgiveness. At least now he will die at peace with the Lord."

"And with you?"

"And with me, I hope."

"How much did you tell him?" Ellen asked.

"Everything." She gazed at her daughter. "Yes, everything you've guessed. He loves you already, Ellen. And he needs your love in return."

Ellen shook her head. "I pity him, terribly. I was beginning to love him, too, as the uncle I'd missed knowing. But . . ."

"Ellen, you have to understand he wasn't in his right mind when he . . . when it happened. He'd been given drugs, for pain. He drank when the drugs weren't enough."

"How could a man . . . ?" Ellen couldn't say the word. "How could he do that to a fifteen-year-old girl and not know what he was doing?"

"Rage is a terrible thing, Ellen. He felt so much rage—rage at being gassed, at being sick, at losing his girl."

Ellen started to interrupt, but Marianne did not let her. "No, that doesn't make it right, but it does help to make us more able to forgive. Do you understand the difference?"

Ellen nodded. Her mind understood; she just wanted her heart to feel it. "Did he know before he left, about me?"

"No, Ellen. He left that very night. I'm sure he never dreamed there would be a child."

"Maybe you should have left it at that. I think I could face him as your little sister, pretending not to know. I want to love him; he's my father. But you are my mother, and I do love you, and he hurt you so."

"I had to tell him. He needed to know about you, Ellen. You have brought so much joy into my life. He had to have a chance, a little time, to know that joy too. And I wanted him to know that God had brought good from the evil he's dwelt on for so long. To me you are the living proof of God's forgiveness, and Eric, even more than I, needed that proof."

Ellen's eyes filled with tears. "Part of me hates him, Marianne, for what he did to you. But how can I hate him, when but for him I wouldn't exist? You make it sound so easy. God brings good from evil. But if that's true, why does God permit evil to begin with? Where was your God when . . .?"

"I did wonder, for a while," Marianne admitted softly. "And for a long time I wondered what I had done to deserve such punishment. But then you came into my life, and I wondered what I had done to deserve such a blessing. So you see it isn't a matter of what we deserve at all. It is God's infinite wisdom."

"If you hadn't had me, you would have had the same joy with your other children anyway. And if I hadn't been born, well, I wouldn't know what I'd missed, would I?" She laughed ruefully. "I don't understand your God, and I don't understand how you can believe in him, but I envy you."

"All your life, Ellen, and even before you were born, I've prayed that God would keep all this from you, would never let you be hurt by it, or by anything else. Maybe that was wrong. Maybe without pain we can't find joy. Maybe without knowing evil we can't really come to know God."

"Then there should be a lot of good Christians in the world," Ellen snorted.

"I was like you once, before. . . . always went to church and said my prayers. I was younger, and times were different. I guess you'd say I still believed in God, but I didn't really know him until I felt need and, yes, some guilt, too, because I believed, then, that such things didn't happen to good girls. I needed help, and I turned to Jesus."

"But you shouldn't have felt guilty. You weren't to blame."

"I did come to realize that, Ellen, and I'm glad you understand. Eric did do wrong. I can't deny that, but I can forgive it with God's help. He has lived with an overpowering guilt ever since that afternoon. It took him many years, but now he has come to Jesus too."

"Marx said religion was the opiate of the people. Sounds to me like you're agreeing with him."

It was Marianne's turn for the rueful chuckle. "Not opiate, exactly. More like bread and water. We can't live without it."

"I can."

"You admitted you envied me."

"Oh, sure," Ellen agreed. "It would be nice to feel good all the time, about everything. It's all in God's hands; he's taking care of me; everything's going to turn out right in the end. But, Marianne, if everyone felt that way, who'd do the work? Who'd go out and make the world better?"

"Us," Marianne answered without hesitation. "That's the philosophy I live by. God's people do his work. We make it better, but only with his help. No, that isn't right. He makes it better; we're the helpers."

Ellen wasn't ready to be just a helper. "It doesn't work for me. I have to take the responsibility. I can't accept that I am just a cog in God's big assembly line. The only thing I can be sure of, absolutely sure, is myself. I have to have faith in myself."

"Faith in God is, itself, a gift from God, Ellen. And maybe you aren't ready, yet, to receive that gift. Just promise me you'll be open. Don't harden your heart. The time will come."

The children came to them. "The peanuts are all gone," Mark said.

"I am going to call Mom tonight," Marianne told Ellen as she rose from the bench. "Eric was relieved that Gran never knew what happened, and he does want to see her. But, like you, I fear his time is short."

Ellen did not go to see Eric the next day. Part of her still hated him. *But how can I waste these precious hours in hatred?* she reproached herself. *He's already wasted all his life with guilt. Hasn't he paid the penalty, and more?*

The day after that, still uncertain, she dragged herself to the TB ward. When she saw him, she realized he was failing fast. It was almost as if he had been waiting for Marianne's forgiveness. He lay quietly, but reached out for Ellen's hand as soon as he saw her.

"She told me," he whispered hoarsely. "I've been so sorry, for so long for what I did to her." Ellen left her hand in his and felt his feeble grasp as he continued. "But I'm happy about you. Now I know my life has been worth something after all. Something good."

With a trembling hand, he reached up and pulled the isolation mask from her face. Ellen blinked back tears. His eyes, wide, open, blue, so much like her own, Ellen realized, studied her features. He struggled to lift his head from the pillow. "Marianne said she had forgiven me, Ellen. Can you?"

"You're my father," she whispered. "I love you." He dropped back into the pillow, satisfied.

"They'll be here any minute, Eric." she told him then. "Mom and Dad . . ." She paused, remembering. "Carrie and Matt did raise me, and they'll always be Mom and Dad."

He nodded. "Marianne told me that too."

"They'll be here soon—with your mother. I thought you might want some help getting ready. Would you like to get dressed?"

He pointed to the robe that hung on a hook nearby,

and struggled to sit up as she slipped it over his shoulders. She combed the streaked gray-gold hair back from his face. He was terribly pale, but with the tell-tale fever flush on his cheeks.

They heard soft voices in the hall, and Ellen went to the doorway, the mask still dangling around her neck. "Yes, Gran, he's waiting for you."

Anna was nearly as pale as her son. Her feet shuffled. Ellen took her arm and led her to Eric's bed. Neither spoke for several moments. Ellen drew a chair close to the bedside, and Anna dropped into it. Her eyes found Eric's. The look spoke to Ellen of all the years of loneliness and heartache, and it spoke of a joy and gratitude too great for mere words.

"Thank God you've come back," Anna cried.

"Mama."

Ellen drew the drab hospital curtain around the bed and stepped outside. Marianne was in the hall with Matt and Carrie. "They need to be alone, together," Ellen said, and each of them nodded.

"And maybe we do too." Carrie stretched out her arms to hold daughter and granddaughter.

"Are you all right, Ellen?" she asked gently. "Finding out all of this, all of a sudden?"

"I'm fine, Mom." She realized she meant it. "Just think how lucky I am. Two mothers and two fathers. And so much love."

It must have been an hour before Anna came out. "He's sleeping," she explained. "I'm afraid he's much too tired and sick to go home. I wanted him to see them all—Will, Tim, Harry, Adele. And the little ones he's never had a chance to know. He wanted to hear all about them. But he's so sick."

"The farm's in good hands with Will and Harry there," Matt assured her. "So we can stay here with you as long as necessary."

"You can all stay at my apartment, Gran," Marianne offered. "So you can come and visit every day."

"Marianne, thank you so much," Anna sighed. "And not just for the place to stay."

Marianne and Ellen exchanged glances.

"Did you think I didn't know, all these years?" the old woman asked. "From the day Matt and Carrie came back to Soledad with Ellen in their arms, I knew why my son had left. I'm his mother. How could I not love him, and forgive him anything? But you, Marianne. For you to forgive, and ease his last days by your forgiveness—how can I ever thank you enough for that?"

Chapter Thirteen

*E*ric died early in July, surrounded by the family he
thought he had lost forever and the daughter he had never
known. Two weeks later Ellen was capped, and enlisted
in the Army Nurse Corps. In early December, after working a few months in Oakland, she received orders to go
to Kentucky for training as a flight nurse. But first, she
spent her short leave in Soledad.

A steady rain had been falling for two days. The soil
of the valley drank it eagerly, and turned ebony. The wet
green lettuce and cabbage and carrots sown a few weeks
before glowed like so many emeralds when the sun
slipped, now and again, from behind the clouds.

Inside, the farm kitchen was warm and bright. Matt
had remodeled it when crop prices went up. Carrie kept
the red and blue spatter-patterned linoleum glowing with
wax, and scoured the white grout on the red-trimmed
countertop every week. She had softened the fashionably
white cupboard doors with bright red geranium decals and

topped the venetian blinds with red and white checked valances.

"You shouldn't have postponed your Thanksgiving dinner just for me," Ellen protested, as Carrie leaned into the oven, turkey baster in hand. "Mmmm, but it does smell good."

"We didn't." Carrie stood up, red-faced from the oven heat. "Everybody had their own dinners, pretty much. Adele's and Harry's family were at Anna's place. Will and Irene and Tim and Nancy stayed home. Liz and Ted both went to their in-laws. Marianne was needed in San Francisco at the U.S.O. party for the servicemen. So Matt and I decided to just have some fried chicken here and not make a big fuss."

Carrie reached for the kettle of potatoes as Ellen finished peeling them. "I think that's enough." She filled the kettle with water and set it on the stove. "I'm really getting off easy. We're going to count this as Thanksgiving and Christmas both, and let Liz have a turn at hosting the Christmas circus."

Ellen laughed. "Circus it is—more so every year I guess. How many little kids are there now?"

"You think I can keep count? Isn't it wonderful that they all still live close by, though?" Carrie's voice dropped. "Of course there's Sam and Johnnie and Joe, all overseas. And Paul, trapped in China. Eric, back so suddenly and now gone forever. And you, in Kentucky for Christmas and God knows where after that."

"But we're all safe, so far at least. So we do still have a lot to be thankful for, Mom. And maybe by next year . . ."

"Maybe. The war news does sound better, but it's a

long way from over. By the way, did you know Ron is home?"

"Ron? Was he hurt?"

"No. He says he had a guardian angel on his shoulder. So many men he knew were shot down. But he got through his twenty-five missions, so he's home on leave. I think he's going to some air base in Texas, then, as an instructor."

"His mother must be so relieved."

Carrie nodded. "Sometimes I almost feel guilty about Ted. He does, too, but it isn't that he didn't want to go to war. It wasn't his fault he hurt that knee in high school. And we do need him here. Matt, Will, and Tim aren't old men, but, well, you do slow down a bit when you get into your fifties and sixties. Your Uncle Harry works sixty hours a week as it is. So does Ted, for that matter."

"McLean-Hanlon Enterprises—it sounds impressive, doesn't it?" Ellen had been surprised by the decision of Matt and her uncles, Will and Harry, to incorporate the family farms.

"Especially when you consider what we all started with," Carrie agreed. "Nearly a thousand acres, and we started with just Papa's ten and Matt's twenty."

"Where do you get the help? Just managing the business must be a full-time job for them."

"Actually that's why they decided to incorporate. It makes it easier to divide the management duties."

"But who does the planting and harvesting with the Japanese gone, and the Filipinos and the Okies and all the valley kids in the army or working in war plants?"

"Kids," Carrie answered. "School kids. They do work

hard, God love them, though they need a lot of supervision. And women. Last year the packing crew was almost entirely women; a lot of them picked too."

"Gee," Ellen teased. "I'm sure glad I got an education. One summer in the sheds was one summer too many for me."

"I'm not sure I agree with you." Carrie patted Ellen's arm. "I think I'd rather have you working in a packing shed than up there in an airplane, especially in a war zone."

"Now, Mom. I'm a nurse. Hospitals and medical evacuation planes are off limits."

"Hospitals, maybe. But those planes? I don't know what keeps them up there anyhow, and you can't tell me putting a red cross on the tail does that much good. Still . . ." she paused as a car door slammed out front, signaling the arrival of the first of their guests. "Still," she concluded, "we're awfully proud of you."

After dinner Ellen called the Stephenses. *It's the neighborly thing to do*, she rationalized, not admitting how much she wanted to see Ron again. His letters had been less frequent lately. Maybe the thing with the English Ellen was more serious than he'd said. *But he's back now, and without her, I gather.*

Ron sounded pleased to hear from her. "You're leaving the end of the week for what, Ellen? Flight training! I thought you hated airplanes."

He came over Friday afternoon. The spell of rain had ended, and they put on sweaters and sat on the Hanlons' porch swing. "I'm still astonished that you volunteered for flight duty," Ron told her.

"I never said I hated airplanes," she protested. "I said, once, when I was young and idealistic, that wanting to risk one's life flying airplanes was childish. Back then I thought war was a game little boys liked to play too."

"Maybe you were right, Ellen."

"How can you say that? Now, when we're fighting desperately for all we believe in?"

"I guess I meant that's how it was then. When I remember how I thought it would be. That was childish, Ellen. I thought war would be heroic, noble, exciting."

"You don't think so anymore, do you?"

He shook his head, slowly. "No. It's dirty, smelly, bloody. It's boys going out to kill other boys and coming back old men—or not coming back at all."

"But with a purpose," she said fervently.

"Yes," he admitted. "There has to be a purpose, or we wouldn't do it. We would never go out day after day and drop those bombs. We couldn't bear to see our best friends spiral down in a ball of fire or watch a country burn up under us, if we didn't believe there was a purpose. But when this is over, will we find a better way?"

"We have to, or all you have done, all of you, will be for nothing," she said softly. "We can't let that happen."

"I'm glad you understand, Ellen. My mother, my kid brother, most of the people who haven't been to war don't know Sherman was right when he said 'war is hell.' But you do understand. It's almost as if you'd already been there. But oh, how I wish you weren't going."

"What else can I do?" She said it not as a question, but as a simple statement of fact. "I didn't want this war.

133

You know that. But it was forced on us, and I can't sit back and ignore it."

"I almost wanted it," he admitted. "But now I'd give anything for it never to have started. Aren't you even going to say you told me so?" he asked, forcing a hint of his old boyish teasing into his somber adult voice.

They rocked for a while in silence, she at one end of the swing and he at the other. "Ellen," he asked at last, "has anything else changed?"

"Lots of things." She looked at him, puzzled.

"Between us?" he asked intently. "We seem to have settled our differences about the war. How about the rest? Are we still friends?" He turned sideways on the swing to face her.

"Ron, we'll always be friends." The question took her by surprise. She had not thought of Ron as anything but a friend in years. *Surely he isn't carrying a torch. After all, he's the one who broke it off.* "What happened to the other Ellen?" she found herself asking.

"Nothing," he told her. "We enjoyed each other's company, like you enjoyed Ken's, I gather. And then I came home."

"I was in love with Ken." She thought about it for a minute. *Funny, but his name has scarcely crossed my mind in months.* "Or I thought I was, anyhow," she added. "He's married, you know, to a Nisei girl."

He drew back into the corner of the swing. "I never even thought I was in love with my English Ellen."

"Ron, what do you expect me to say? I like you a lot. I always have. Probably, if I were still little Ellen Hanlon of Soledad, we'd have gotten married one day. But I left

134

the valley and I did go out into the world, and it changed me. I'll never be that same girl again."

She studied him as he rocked beside her. He had never been strikingly handsome. His tan had faded, in the English fog no doubt. His face was thinner, but it was still a good, trustworthy face. His hazel eyes were still gentle, but little worry-lines had formed at the corners. His wide mouth was firm without hardness, his jaw strong. His dress uniform gave stature to a short, somewhat stocky frame, and his chest wore the battle ribbons and silver wings with deserved pride.

"And you aren't the same boy, either," she told him. "You're a man now. I like that man, but then, I always liked you, even loved you—and I do love you, Ron, like a brother . . ."

"Thanks," he muttered almost too softly for her to hear.

"Even if it were more, I'm still not what you want, Ron, not unless you've changed in other ways. You said, yourself, that God was the most important person in your life. A girl doesn't want to take second place.

"I thought Ken and I could make it work," she went on. "We thought alike about a lot of things, but in the end he was right to marry the girl his family approved of, the girl he'd grown up with."

"We grew up together."

"There's always your mother."

"Oh, I could handle my mother and her silly, baseless gossip."

Baseless. She recalled one very important change in her life since she had last talked to Ron. *Well, it will stay*

135

baseless as far as he is concerned, for Marianne's sake if not mine, and for the rest of the family.

"Ron, what came between us was much more than your mother's disapproval. And it wasn't my fault either. It was important to you, and you made it clear a long time ago that you couldn't consider marriage to a girl who didn't share your faith. I'm sorry, but I can't change what I believe. I respect your belief; I don't ask you to change. But can you give me the same privilege?"

He stood and his body seemed to sag as his eyes avoided hers. Then he squared his shoulders and looked down at her. "Ellen, no matter who I marry, or if I ever marry at all, the most important thing in my life has always been my Lord, and no, that hasn't changed. The past year—the fear, the destruction, the death—it's all made Christ even more real to me. I guess I hoped the war, or your sister, or something, might have drawn you back to him."

Ron offered his hand. She took it, stood, and walked with him to his car. "Still friends?" he whispered.

"Friends, always," she promised.

Ellen went to church the next Sunday to please her parents. Ron, she knew, would not be fooled by her presence. Still, he'd be there, and though they were destined to be only friends, she treasured that friendship.

Everyone in the little congregation fussed over the visitors, both returning pilot and newly commissioned army nurse. Even Mrs. Stephens hugged Ellen and assured her she would be praying for her safety "up there in those airplanes."

I guess she's decided I'm no threat to her son, Ellen reflected, as she sat upright in the stiff pew. *Funny, her vicious gossip turns out to be true after all, and so what?* Ellen wondered briefly if Ron would care, and concluded it would matter no more to him than it ever had. *He doesn't care what his mother thinks. All he cares about is what God thinks.*

Ellen glanced across the aisle to where he sat between his mother and his kid brother. She caught him looking at her, and quickly dropped her eyes. *We could be more than friends,* she admitted, *if I were willing to play the part. But why would I ever want a man I had to lie to get, and live a lie to keep? And why would I want a man who cares more about an intangible concept of God than about a real, flesh and blood woman?*

Chapter Fourteen

The big C-47 Skytrain was crammed with crates marked Spam, Powdered Eggs, and Cigarettes. Ellen and another flight nurse sat on stiff jump seats just behind the cockpit. Peering around the heads of the pilot and co-pilot, Ellen could see several other transport planes playing hide-and-seek among the dark clouds.

"I told my mother I'd be perfectly safe," she confided to her companion, Cathy. "I told her medical evac planes were marked, and nobody would attack them."

Cathy shivered. "I thought that, too, when I volunteered. Now they tell us that when we're headed east these are just ordinary military supply planes, and that makes us fair game."

"Not to worry, ladies," the lanky Texas pilot drawled. "I ain't had even one plane shot out from under me yet."

"Yet," Ellen echoed.

"You'll get used to it," the co-pilot promised with a flat, eastern twang. "First trip's always the hardest."

"At least going back we'll be too busy to worry," Ellen reasoned. "Just one nurse with fourteen wounded men."

"It scares me," Cathy admitted. "I mean, what if something goes wrong with no doctor around?"

"I think that's the main reason I wanted to do it. It's a big responsibility, sure, but I didn't spend five years in school just to follow some doctor's orders. I'm well trained. I'm intelligent. I can handle it, and I look forward to proving I can."

The Texan guffawed, but the Yankee turned around. "Good girl," he told her. "If I do get mine, I'd like to wake up and find you at my bedside."

"How come it took you five years?" the Texan asked. "My sister's a nurse, and she only went for two."

"I have a university degree." Ellen hoped the patronizing tone hit home with Texas without hurting Cathy's feelings. Since knowing May, Ellen was trying not to think she was any better than the more traditionally trained nurses. "I always intended to do more than just ward nursing."

"Then why not go all the way, if you don't like to take orders?" Texas pushed. "Some girls . . ." He stressed the words meaningfully. "Some girls figure they can be as good doctors as men."

Ellen ignored his condescension. "Money, mostly. Medical school is expensive." She paused, thoughtfully. "Who knows? Maybe when this war's over I will go to med school."

Yank gave Ellen an approving grin, but Cathy looked almost as shocked as Texas. "It's so hard, Ellen."

"I've got the grades. Why should it be any harder for me than for anybody else?"

They were still a thousand miles from England, and the conversation might be stimulating, but it was not doing much to calm their nerves. "Let's change the subject," Ellen offered. "Tell us about England."

"Yes," Cathy agreed. "We sort of expected to be sent to the Pacific."

"You won't believe the English, girls," Yank told them. "They've had over three years of Churchill's 'blood, sweat, toil, and tears' and they're still going strong. Meat's scarce; gas—they call it 'petrol' by the way—is scarce; sugar's scarce."

"That's what hurts them the most, to hear them tell it," Tex offered.

"A friend of mine mentioned that too," Ellen recalled. "He wrote that they complained more about giving up their sweets than about being bombed."

"Gentleman friend? Rats! I might have known."

"Family friend," Ellen assured Yank. "Ron's a bomber pilot."

"Ouch. That's tough. I gather he's been lucky so far."

"He's been very lucky. He put in his twenty-five missions, and now he's in Texas as an instructor."

"That ain't just luck," Tex exploded. "That's a raving miracle. Survived twenty-five missions and then got sent straight to heaven."

They all roared with laughter at Tex's pride. "I hate to tell you," Ellen felt compelled to inform him, "but Ron prefers California." She sobered. "He did call it a miracle, though. Are the losses really so high?"

"He probably got the worst of it." Tex was serious now too. "At first it was pretty awful. The top brass insisted on daylight bombing over Germany for accuracy. The fighters couldn't go that far, so they sent those Flying Forts out alone. If the Luftwaffe didn't get you, the flak did. They finally had to stop it. After six or eight months we were running out of planes."

"Not to mention crews," Yank interjected. "Those were the guys who got in before Pearl Harbor and were already trained. They've started up the daylight bombing again with the new guys, but now they've got fighter escort."

"Yeah, and you got to admit the beating the RAF gave the Germans a year ago helped too," Tex conceded.

"I thought last winter, well, since it's almost spring I should say winter before last, was the worst of the blitz," Cathy commented.

"Oh, it was," Yank agreed. "You'll see soon enough the damage that was done. But eventually the English won. The RAF fighter pilots shot down the German fighters something like two to one. They downed so many of Hitler's bombers that the Germans still haven't caught up—never will, now. So it's our turn to bomb their cities, and bomb them until they'll be eternally grateful to surrender."

"Didn't you say we were still bombing in daylight?" Ellen inquired.

"Well, yes, day and night both. The English still favor nights, maybe because they know just how frightening it is to be awakened night after night by air raid sirens. We go mostly in daylight, so we can pinpoint our targets. But like Yank says, it's not so dangerous now."

"Don't worry, though," the co-pilot assured them quietly. "There'll be plenty of wounded for you to tend."

"There's more to it than that, isn't there?" Ellen probed. "It isn't just more pilots being sent to England and more planes."

"No, and no doubt 'Jerry' knows as much about it as we do, maybe more. There's a build-up, a big one. There are U.S. camps all over the country. You see more American uniforms than British, not to mention the Canadians. It's all supposed to be hush-hush, but no way you can hide a hundred thousand or so troops and the logistics that go with it. We're headed for France, and soon."

The men had been right about the build-up. As the two nurses rode in a jeep across England's rolling, emerald green countryside, Ellen could not avoid contrasting it to the Salinas Valley. "At home," she explained to Cathy, "the green isn't continuous. The fields themselves are green, but in between it's brown. Even this time of year, unless it's been an awfully wet winter, it's only maybe a little greenish except where it's irrigated."

Cathy, the Midwesterner, shook her head. "I guess it's less risky than the way we do it in Ohio. When we have a dry summer our farmers suffer. But it still seems funny that people spend so much money on irrigation instead of farming where it rains."

"It's rich soil," Ellen defended. "It does produce." She surveyed the scene around her. "The towns are a lot closer together here too. Seems like there's a little village every two or three miles."

In between, almost like the ordered row-crops of her valley, grew neat rows of khaki tents. The Union Jack flew alongside the Stars and Stripes, but the camps were unquestionably American G.I. Except for the green of the grass around them, the camps weren't unlike the overflow sprawl at Hunter-Leggett or Fort Ord back home.

The olive drab jeep turned off the paved two-lane highway onto a narrow graveled lane and pulled to a stop at a sentry booth. The guard checked their orders, saluted smartly, grinned at the new nurses, and waved them through.

This was obviously a more permanent encampment. Low, hump-backed Quonset hut barracks surrounded a carefully maintained airstrip. Their jeep bounced along a less well-tended roadway and stopped before the one building on the base that had been painted. Its roof was still bright white, which set off its blazing red cross. "Here you are, ladies. Your home away from home." The driver hopped out and gallantly handed them down as if the open jeep were a limousine. "Major Schaeffer's the head nurse. Her office is inside and to the left."

They presented their orders, and Major Schaeffer extended a hand to each of them. "We're glad to have you. Our hospital can always use more help. I'll show you around myself, and then you can have the rest of the day to unpack and get settled into your quarters."

Ellen paused at a bulletin board near the back entrance to the building, and glanced around. The building was incredibly simple. The hallway cut the long, low structure in two and connected front and back entrances. Narrower halls ran to Ellen's right and left, forming four equal rectangles in all. Compared to the maze of buildings, wings, and annexes at Fort Miley and Oakland, it would be a cinch to find her way around here.

The major was explaining the assignment lists on the bulletin board. "As you can see, we're moving you around a bit at first, so you'll get acquainted with both surgery and the medical wards. Incidentally, your coming will give each of the girls who have been here for several months some leave time. Any questions?"

"I understood we'd be working in a base hospital between flights, Major. But we will be flying back and forth with wounded men, won't we? Will those assignments be posted here too?"

"Usually, unless there's an emergency." Major Schaeffer lowered her voice. "There won't be many flights, girls, not for a while anyhow. We don't have that many men who require evacuation."

She must have noticed their puzzled frowns. "No, the army doesn't make mistakes. One of these days you'll be using all your skills, and a few you didn't know you had. I don't know how soon, but it's obvious we're building up for something big, probably in early summer when the weather improves. Meantime, we'll keep you busy enough here."

She smiled then. "And, of course, it's your duty, after hours, to keep up morale. I don't have to tell you the rules, and I hope I don't have to remind you about behavior becoming an officer. On the other hand, we aren't real, real fussy about fraternization."

Chapter Fifteen

*I*t was a bright, clear spring morning. "Wonderful," Cathy was saying as she and Ellen walked across the dew-dampened grass from their quarters to the base hospital. "I've never seen a place where it was gray so much of the time."

Ellen laughed. "It's just like home."

"I thought you came from farm country. And don't try to tell me crops grow without sunshine."

"Maybe the sun's more intense when it does shine in Soledad," Ellen explained. "Anyhow, it only rains half the time, even in the winter. From April to October it scarcely rains at all. The evening and morning fog provides some moisture for the crops, but even so it's sunny most afternoons."

"Seems like it's been raining in England every day since we flew in."

"Seems like it." Ellen sniffed the faintly salty breeze. "Actually, by home I meant San Francisco. People do say it rains all the time there, but that's a slight exaggeration. In the summer it's cool and damp, but the real rain comes in the winter. Even then there are lots of sunny days like this. We live for them."

Her ears picked up the sounds of revving engines from the far end of the base runway. "Maybe fair weather isn't such good news," she murmured. "They're going out."

Cathy nodded, and they picked up their pace. They'd been in England for nearly three weeks with no break in the pea-soup weather until today. The men they met at the Officers' Club were getting testy from inaction. The girls wondered why they'd been sent here at all when so many men were fighting in the mountains of Italy and in the disease-ridden morass of the South Pacific.

The tension in the little hospital was palpable. "Get the charts ready on all the patients in the medical ward," Ellen was told. "Colonel Palmer will be reviewing them all."

"All?"

"SOP," the head nurse snapped. Then, noting Ellen's puzzled look, her voice softened. "Standard operating procedure. We release everybody we can before a big raid. We want to free up every possible bed."

The morning, which Ellen would have expected to be interminably long and filled with worried expectation, passed in a whirlwind of action. Supplies were inventoried and stacked at ready. Every airman and every ground crew member who had been sick enough for hospitalization the day before was scrutinized. If he did not need constant nursing care or observation, back to the barracks he went. *And eagerly*, Ellen realized.

Every surgical instrument in the place was sterilized and stacked in the two operating rooms. The newly emptied beds were hastily remade. The place that had seemed so unbelievably relaxed the day before was taut with the electric tension. And everyone listened.

By mid-afternoon the first distant drones came. Drivers sprang into the ambulances that stood by the hospital entrance, and the nurses scrambled into their assigned places. The roar of truck engines mingled with the approaching hum of the bombers.

The first planes to arrive were intact—the ones that had escaped both flak and Luftwaffe relatively unscathed. Their crews climbed down and stretched wearily, stiff from sitting or crouching in their cramped cockpits, gun turrets, and bomb bays. They pushed helmets from sweaty foreheads as they staggered off, shoulders slumped, for debriefing.

The motors that approached later did not hum so smoothly. Their engines sputtered as they straggled toward the runway. Their landings were rough, some coming in with tires missing or flat. Some had only three or even two of their four propellers turning. One plane swerved sideways because the hand on the stick was too weak to hold it on course.

The ambulances drove onto the tarmac to meet those planes. Corpsmen pulled up unsteady ladders and handed down unsteady men. It was Ellen's first sight of war. Asked later what her thoughts were, she could only respond honestly, "I never had time to think."

It was dark when the last flesh wound had been stitched, the last new amputee sedated, the last man beyond saving covered for his final sleep. Cathy and Ellen walked back toward their quarters. "I'll never think the sunny days are the good ones again," Ellen sighed.

April brought more fair weather. Nearly every day some of the planes went out. Most days Ellen, Cathy, and the other army nurses found ample challenge, and more, for their skills. Ellen made two flights back to the United States with wounded men who could probably have been treated as well in England. Still, the planes had to go west to pick up more men and more supplies. *But I really don't see where they can put any more stuff on this little fortress island*, she thought.

Both times she returned on VIP flights with high-ranking officers. April brought more planes, too, and more men and more nurses. "Everyone knows the invasion is coming," they told each other. The only questions were when and where.

"The Germans probably know more about that than we do," Ellen remarked to Captain Jim Roberts one off-duty Sunday afternoon. "I suppose 'when' depends on the weather. Where? The English Channel isn't that long, is it? They must have the whole French coast armed to the teeth by now."

"Mmm," the pilot muttered. "That's where we come in. We've been hammering them almost every day, and we'll keep it up as long as this weather holds—probably in the fog, too, if we have to. We're softening up the whole stretch. I feel kind of sorry for the French."

"Don't you think they know why the bombing's been stepped up? They must be so excited."

"I'll bet they are. But while we try to hit fuel dumps,

coastal fortifications, railroads—especially railroads—you know we have to be killing Frenchmen as well. That's the awful thing about this kind of war. So many little people, innocent people, get clobbered."

"Hasn't that always been true of war, Jim? Even in the Middle Ages, fields that should have been growing crops were trampled. Women and children starve in sieges; your everyday foot soldier, the cannon-fodder, is usually a poor man."

"Yes, but this is even worse. You're lucky, Ellen. You weren't here during the Blitz. The 'Battle of Britain' has pretty much been won now, and you won't see anything like it again because Hitler doesn't have enough planes left. But this is my second tour. A year ago I was here, and I saw it. I happened to be in London during a couple of air raids. Now every time I go up I remember the kids crying and the old people grubbing through the ruins trying to pick up the pieces of their lives. Ellen, when we've finished up this mess and hung Herr Hitler, we've got to find a way to keep it from happening again."

"That's what Ron said," she reflected.

"Ron? So you're not so fancy-free after all."

"Oh, it's nothing like that," she told him a little too quickly. "He's a hometown boy. We went together for a while when we were kids, but now we're just good friends. He was over here a year ago. I saw him last fall while he was home on leave."

"Flyboy?"

"Bomber pilot, like you. Ron Stephens. You didn't happen to know him, did you?"

His grin answered. "Ron Stephens! Lucky Stephens!

Small world. We were in the same squadron based up north."

"Lucky?"

Jim nodded. "That's what we called him after the first ten missions or so. It was really rough over here then, Ellen. Sometimes we lost half our planes, or more, on one raid. Not that Ron called it luck." Jim paused, thoughtfully. "Maybe he was right, come to think of it. Maybe it was a guardian angel riding his wing, but he sure had a knack of getting his plane back in one piece. Got so we'd all ask him, especially before a tricky one, to say a prayer for us too."

"No doubt he did. Even without your asking, probably. Ron's always been the praying kind."

Jim poked at the cigarette butt Ellen had dropped into the ashtray and eyed the mug of cold beer in front of her. "Was that the problem? I mean, you're a decent girl and all that, but . . ."

"I used to be almost as bad as Ron," she admitted, smiling. "Went to church every Sunday, said grace before every meal. If my folks knew that I smoked or had a beer now and then, they would probably disown me. But I went away to college, and, well, I guess I outgrew that 'old time religion.'"

"Around here it tends to work the other way. They say there are no atheists in foxholes. I don't think there are many in bomber squadrons either."

"It's funny, in a way," she reflected. "I went to college and it seemed like nobody there, except Ron of course, read the Bible or prayed. I don't know just when I stopped believing all of it. I just did. Marianne, my sister . . ." She chuckled. "Would you believe I have a sister who is a Salvation Army officer? Anyhow, my sister said once that I'd lost my faith because I never had to exercise it. I never really needed God."

"Your sister just may have hit the bull's-eye," Jim told her. "A few months of action, and most of us, if we don't believe in God by then, at least wish we did. I guess I'm with you. It's hard to make sense out of that line Ron used. If God loves us so much, why does he let us get into such horrible messes? But it would be a lot easier, up there, if I knew someone was watching out for me."

She drank a few sips of the beer and pushed it aside. "Talking about Ron and Marianne must tickle my conscience," she muttered.

"Just keep spending your evenings with me. I'll cure you," Jim assured her.

But she pushed her chair back and stood. "Tomorrow is another busy day. And I need my beauty sleep."

There was no question about it. The long-awaited invasion of France was close. Waves of planes had already been ferried across the Atlantic and sat wing tip to wing tip on the hastily expanded tarmac. The men were doubling up in the barracks. Ellen and Cathy were already old-timers among the nurses, drilling newcomers in the practice runs they crowded in between the all-too-real forays.

Ellen left in early May on what had become, already, a routine Atlantic crossing. Her C-47 Skytrain had its full complement of fourteen stretcher cases, mostly amputees going home for rehabilitation.

The plane flew dark, for safety, and Ellen checked the men's vital signs and inspected bandaged stumps by flashlight. The crises she had half hoped to contend with seldom occurred because the wounded were kept in England until their conditions were stable.

She was in the cabin, reading to one of her patients when she heard the unexpected crackle of the radio. She had not understood what was said, but the young gunner, going home sightless, asked what was happening, and she went forward to find out.

The co-pilot pointed below and moved to the side so she could lean over his shoulder to see the battle.

She couldn't see the thin periscope, but the co-pilot assured her it was there. She saw the pair of destroyers move away from the convoy, circling their prey even as it must be stalking its own—the troopships, tankers, merchant vessels low in the water under their heavy supply loads.

A troopship had been hit; she was certain of it. But at least the submarine was found by one of the destroyers, thanks, in part, anyway, to the pilot's warning. The rest of the convoy got through.

On the rest of the long flight the men slept mostly, stirring when the plane set down for refueling in Iceland or Greenland or Labrador. "Are we there, nurse? Are we home yet?"

"Just pulled into the gas station," she would assure them. "But everything's fine. You'll be stateside before you know it."

The return trip was worse. Then there was time to think—too much time, and she thought about Marianne.

Always serene, always so self-confident. Okay, so you call it faith, she apologized silently. *And Eric.* Ellen had put on a good front, she assured herself. She never let him know how mixed her feelings were toward him. She had let him die at peace, at long last, with himself.

But my father was weak. He was cruel, and he was weak. Has Eric left some mark on me, some bad seed, that will find its way out? Matt thought so, she suspected. *He was always so strict with me. Was it because Matt was afraid of that inherent, and maybe inherited, weakness?*

As the plane winged through the darkness, she reread letters and recalled happier times. She was glad Ron was safe in Texas, although he sounded impatient with the training routine. And she thought of Kim and Ken. She hoped Ken and Midori were happy. Kim had been released from the camp at Manzanar at last and was finally finishing her nurses' training.

But it was a long trip back to England. When Ellen had analyzed her newly discovered heritage to exhaustion and reread the last letters from home, there was nothing else to do but worry. She still had half a day of wondering if the sturdy *Gooney Bird* would hold up one more time, and if it would escape the ever present danger of icing. As they approached the North Sea, Ellen worried lest a stray German battleship would spot them within range of its big guns or a Luftwaffe patrol would cross their path.

The ocean was not empty below them; it never was. Convoys came in sight, were left behind; new ones spotted, and passed. "Almost a railroad, isn't

155

it?" the pilot commented. "A railroad, right across the ocean.

"Keep a sharp lookout," he warned his co-pilot. "There are still U-boats out there." Then he turned to Ellen. "That's the one thing we break radio silence for," he reminded her.

When Ellen returned to the base, she found that still another bomber squadron had been crammed onto it. "Fresh in from Texas," the corporal told her as he gave her a lift to her quarters in a bouncy jeep. "Except for the major. He's an old hand, they tell me. Was here last year, and actually asked to come back for the grand finale. Scuttlebutt is he's pretty special. Guys around here say they used to call him 'Lucky.'"

There are probably a thousand 'Luckys' in the United States Air Corps, she told herself. "Don't happen to know his last name, do you?" Her own eagerness surprised her. "I have an old friend they used to call that—though he was still a captain the last I knew."

"Don't know his name, but I expect he's over at the Officers' Club right now renewing some old friendships. Want to stop there and take a look-see?"

She shrugged. "Why not?"

She figured if it were really Ron he would be with Jim Roberts and the handful of other 'old-timers.' She had not spotted them yet, when a couple of other nurses hailed her. "Ellen. Over here. How was the trip?"

Ron looked up at the sound of her name, and she saw the comfortably familiar face. He stretched out arms still clothed in the leather of his flight jacket. "Ellen, what luck. What incredible luck."

She turned, hurrying toward the outstretched arms. But they fell before she reached him. Only his hands reached out to her and clasped her own.

The kiss that half the crowded room was obviously expecting didn't come. They were still just friends. *Nothing had changed when we saw each other last winter. Why should anything have changed now?*

She congratulated him on his promotion; he told her he was glad to see her, "Though not necessarily under these circumstances." His old buddies drifted off, obviously assuming they wanted to be alone, but that was impossible in the crowded club.

"We could go out and get some fresh air," Ellen suggested. If he heard her, he ignored her.

"So," he said, as he might have to someone he had just met, "how do you like flying the shuttle?"

"I just got back from a trip to Washington," she told him. "We took some amputees and head injuries to Walter Reed. Flew back in a powder keg—literally."

He shuddered. "They shouldn't do that. It isn't right putting women in that kind of danger. Why, if you ever ran into a German patrol plane coming in . . ." He reached out as if to touch her face, but his fingers stopped short. "Ellen, you shouldn't be in danger."

"Why not? We can't afford to fly back empty." She protested his gallantry, though she was touched by it. "Ron, this is our war too. All this idea of the big, brave men going off to war and we delicate little women keeping the home fires burning is history. No," she corrected, "it's myth."

"All the same, good as it is to see you again, I wish you

were back in Soledad, safe." He stared at her, as if he were memorizing her familiar features. At last he sighed. "If you just got in from a ten-hour flight, you must be exhausted. I'll walk you to your quarters."

Chapter Sixteen

Ron's crew was, for the most part, fresh out of flight training. For a few days he flew them on training sorties, until they, too, joined the constant stream of departing and incoming bombers who gave the French coast little respite that May.

Thanks to the faltering German Air Force, Ellen's duties remained relatively light, though the hospital was in a constant state of readiness. Ellen was surprised at the effect Ron's actual closeness had on her, and the distance between them of which it was such a persistent reminder. He was only a few hundred yards away, and knowing that was reassuring. Yet he was really no nearer than he had been for . . . how long? Four years.

It was good to know her best friend was there—a trusted ear to talk to, a strong shoulder to cry on, a quick mind to spar with. He was all that, but something in her wanted more. Besides, he didn't seem to care to be alone with her. *Not that he's ignoring me*, she insisted. *It's just that he's so busy.*

It had only been three days, though it seemed like more. Holding her supper tray, Ellen looked around the Officer's Mess and brightened when she saw his cheerful wave. Neighbors murmured knowingly and edged over, making room for her next to him at the long table.

"I wondered if we'd ever get a chance to talk," he said, the familiar boyish grin cracking the older, firmer, unfamiliar lips.

What about the other night? she wondered.

"I called your quarters a couple of times," he was saying, "but I guess you had night duty. I was beginning to think I'd have to go back to writing letters."

"That might not work either." She chuckled—the girlish chuckle she feared she had lost forever. "There was one waiting for me when I got in the other day. You'd mailed it over a month ago from Texas. By the way, I got the impression that you were spending the rest of the war there. What happened?"

"I volunteered." Some of the other men at the table laughed, but Ron shook off the Air Force humor. "I did, really. There are plenty of men with wives and children who know just as much as I do about steering Flying Fortresses to targets and back. I felt I belonged back here, in action. Those kids . . ." He gestured to a table nearby, where several of the new men sat. "They needed me here."

He walked her back toward the nurses' quarters. They talked mostly about home and the news the long-delayed letters from their parents had brought. The spring breeze carried the smell of freshly tilled earth, and sitting on the wooden steps of the makeshift barracks was almost like being on the Hanlons' porch swing back in Soledad.

"Imagine, with all those thousands of square miles and millions of people, someone smuggling good news about Paul out of China," Ellen was telling him. "It's like a miracle."

"Yes, but God does have a way of working miracles when we really need them. Tough about your cousin, Joe, though," Ron told her.

Carrie's letter to Ellen had brought both good news and bad. Uncle Will's son, Joe, who had been a carrier-based fighter pilot in the Pacific, was missing.

"Still, you never can tell, Ellen. A lot of the guys who go down do get picked up. You might hear in the next letter that Joe is safe after all, or maybe in a Japanese POW camp. Not that that would be good." He gazed for a few moments toward the massed planes on the darkened field. "Bad as the stories are about the German POW camps . . ." He let it dangle. "Still, 'Missing in Action' is better than the alternative."

"That's what Mom said." *Mom.* No one knew the truth but Carrie, Matt, Gran, and Marianne. And none of them wanted to talk about it. Suddenly she wanted, very much, to talk about her family. "I love them all so, Ron. They're so solid and reliable. I used to think, so long ago . . ."

She laughed to herself. "Was it only last winter? But that was a long time ago, wasn't it, before I came here? I used to think nothing would ever touch that sturdy clan of Salinas Valley farmers. Now Joe's gone, probably. Sam's in the South Pacific too, and Johnny in Italy. But back then, even though I loved them, and I knew they loved me, I wasn't really a part of the family."

"Because you were adopted?" he asked gently. "That never seemed to matter to Matt and Carrie."

"Oh, no, Ron. They were always so good to me. But, well, I felt, in my heart, that it wasn't the same."

"There's nothing like facing our own mortality to bring people together, is there?" She realized he had taken her hand, and she felt the security of home and family in his strong grasp. "Yes, but it's more than that." She had not intended to reveal Marianne's secret, but she had always been able to share secrets with Ron. *Even when we were dating,* she realized. *We were best friends even then.* "Ron, something happened before I left for flight training. I need to talk about it, and there hasn't been anyone . . ."

A shadow crossed his face, but a gentle smile chased it away. "Here I am."

"Ron, back in Soledad when we were kids, you heard the gossip, didn't you, about me I mean?"

He frowned. "Ellen, there's always gossip in small towns. It didn't mean anything."

"Remember, when we were dating, how your mother disapproved of me? I overheard her once . . ."

He nodded slowly. "But Ellen, those were just silly old rumors. Why, back then people always suspected the worst."

"Ron, you must never breathe this to anyone back home—never."

"Of course not," he assured her.

"I know you wouldn't. And there are so few people I can trust. It's about the family. It's made me feel so much closer to them, and yet I couldn't talk about it to any of them. The few who know are too close to it, too involved, to help me sort out my feelings."

"Ellen, I don't know anything, really, but if I can help, if it's only by listening, I'm glad I'm here."

She told him, simply and directly, about Marianne's admission the Thanksgiving before Pearl Harbor. "That long ago." She shook her head. "It seems like only yesterday, and yet so much has happened in these last two years."

"Surely you've accepted it by now.

"I think, between the bits and pieces of overheard gossip and my own girlish imagination, I already knew that Marianne was my mother. I always loved her, and I still do. The problem, the thing I can't seem to deal with, is my father."

She knew, from his sad, tender look, that the gossip had, indeed, been that explicit. "He came back, Ron. I met him totally by accident, at the V.A. Hospital in San Francisco. All I knew then was that he was Gran's long lost son. But he was dying. One thing led to another, and it all came out, the whole ugly story."

Ron didn't argue with her. "Of course it's ugly, but it's long over. Anything your father may have done doesn't make you any less lovely, Ellen. It didn't matter when it was mean, petty gossip. It certainly doesn't matter now."

She unconsciously moved nearer to him. "I know that. And, Ron, I really came to love him, I think, in a way. Certainly I pitied him. He was eaten up with guilt. It was a classic Greek tragedy. It ruined his whole life."

"How sad. He was only your mother's stepbrother—step-uncle." Ron corrected himself. "Why didn't they just get married, if they were in love?"

"They weren't in love, Ron. That's what I can't deal with. Not that I don't believe in chastity before marriage. I do." Did she imagine it, she wondered, or did he seem somehow relieved by her statement? *Why should he care?* "If it had been a simple case of young love, I think I could live with that," she continued. "But Ron, he raped my mother. My father was a drunk, a drug addict, and a rapist."

"And?" He said it only as a mild reproof. "And every person on earth is a sinner. Why should your father be different, Ellen? It's only we human beings who sort behavior into big and little sins."

"It's . . . Ron, it isn't that I don't know how I *ought* to feel. I don't know how I *do* feel. The man I knew for those few weeks couldn't forgive himself for betraying the people who loved him. I felt so sorry for him, and yet, knowing what he did. . . Ron, Marianne was only fifteen years old!"

"What about Marianne?" he asked, as his strong arm casually circled her shoulders. "Does she hate him?"

Ellen felt her burden lighten as she shared it with her friend. "Marianne? She forgives everybody, everything. She even forgives the Japanese for driving her out of China and separating her from Paul. Of course she forgave Eric long ago." Her voice took on an edge of bitterness. "But Marianne just doesn't live in the real world."

Ron was looking at the sky, bright with stars. She

suspected he was praying again. *I wish I could,* she found herself thinking. *If I could pray, maybe I could forgive, too, like Marianne.*

His arm slipped from her shoulders, and his fingertips lifted her face to meet his. "Which world is real, Ellen?" he asked at last. "Marianne's, where people sin, but sins are forgiven? Or the one you want to believe in, where everybody will learn, eventually, not to sin?"

Airplane motors drowned out his words for a few moments, RAF planes, heading out for a night raid. "Or that world we have to go out and live in again tomorrow, that world of hatred and death?"

"Isn't my dream world the one we're fighting for?"

"Is it? Do you really believe that once the Germans and the Japanese are licked mankind will suddenly turn good?"

"I can hope so. I have to hope so."

"It hasn't happened yet. Through all of history that perfect world hasn't come yet."

"Neither has Marianne's holy kingdom. Or yours."

"For her it has." He faced her squarely. "For me, too, Ellen. Oh, not always. I slip." He shifted uneasily on the wooden steps and edged away from her. "I'll bet even Marianne slips once in a while. But God's kingdom has come. Really it has."

She opened her mouth to protest. *How can he say that here, now?* "God's kingdom!" she scoffed.

"Inside his children, Ellen. Inside everyone who will let him in."

"You make it sound so simple. Everything goes back to that, doesn't it?" She stood and reached for the doorknob to the nurses' quarters. "Thanks, Ron, for listening."

"Anytime." He waved as he turned away.

She watched from the open door as he slowly walked toward the officers' barracks. She went inside and tiptoed into the room she shared with Cathy. Her friend stirred and muttered something about her coming back for the night after all.

"Ron's just like my big brother, silly." She snuggled down under the coarse army blanket. *Well, he might as well be.* When she was dating Ken it was so exciting. Her heart still beat more quickly, remembering how Ken's every casual touch had made her tingle. When they had danced, she'd been taut with the thought of what it might be like to be with him, alone, intimate. *Not that I ever would have, but, well, I did think about it. I am a perfectly normal human being after all.*

But good old Christian Ron! She curled up and yawned. *Someday I will meet the right man, probably, but meantime, it's awfully nice to have a best friend around to talk to.*

Chapter Seventeen

I wish I had a weekend pass," Cathy teased. "And someone to go to London with."

"We had a chance to go there together last month," Ellen reminded her as she snapped the clasp on her overnight bag. "You preferred the local pub and the company of a tall, dark, not especially handsome colonel as I recall."

Ellen had been surprised when Ron proposed the London trip. Everyone knows why couples go up to London for the weekend. She smiled, half hoping . . . No, when Ron says sight-seeing, he means sight-seeing. She did not bother to pack the lacy negligee Cathy insisted on lending her.

"I could learn to love London," Ellen breathed, as they craned their necks to see the top of the massive dome of St. Paul's Cathedral the next morning. "If only . . ." She gestured toward the bombed-out brick skeletons sur-

167

rounding Christopher Wren's seventeenth-century masterpiece.

Ron's arm circled her waist. "I know. People lived here, and some died here. But look up. Isn't it, somehow, a symbol, a triumph, the way the cathedral stands there?"

"It's scarred, Ron. See." She pointed to a wing of the massive church, blackened and windowless.

"Like this whole country, Ellen. Scarred, but still standing. Have you any idea what these people have been through?"

"I'm beginning to understand," she whispered. "Ron, why? Why must these things happen?"

"You know why as well as I do," he reminded her. "Come on. I want to show you the Tower of London."

From the ancient tower they walked back across the ruins surrounding the cathedral. They sat for a few minutes in Leicester Square, gay with tulips in the midst of the ashes. Near sunset they walked along the Victoria Embankment and watched as Big Ben's gothic tower cast its long shimmering shadow into the current of the Thames.

"Remember when we were kids," Ellen said softly, "and you were going to travel all over the world building roads and railroads and bridges? I dreamed about going with you to all those places."

"There will be a lot of rebuilding, Ellen."

"Yes, I guess you will be living your dream, won't you?"

"Maybe," he said, carefully avoiding her eyes. "Part of my dream, anyhow."

They returned to the little hotel after supper, and the clerk smiled knowingly as they took the keys to their adjoining rooms. *Let him think anything he wants to*, Ellen told herself.

Ron held the door to Ellen's room for her, and she turned toward him as she entered. "It's been a wonderful day, Ron."

"With wonderful company." He squeezed her hand, but avoided her eyes. "See you in the morning," he said with unexpected brusqueness.

Several days after their return from London, Ellen stood in front of her mirror primping for dinner with Ron. She pushed her short hair into soft waves around her face. She powdered her nose, reached for her rouge, then rejected it and touched her lips lightly with a pale lipstick. Though Ron had been steadfastly brotherly in London, it was good being with him. *Maybe it isn't what Cathy thinks it is; maybe it never will be; but he's good for me.*

She already had plans for Friday evening, but when Ron suggested dinner in the nearby village she broke her date with Jim without a second thought.

At the small restaurant, the jukebox played steadily. Part of the room had been cleared for a small dance floor. Jim had come after all with one of the other nurses. He had joked to Ellen when he saw her with Ron about being stood up for the guy from back home.

Ellen's foot tapped under the scarred table. The songs were sad songs, mostly, about lovers separated by the war. "The world will always welcome lovers," the refrain drifted through the room, "as time goes by."

"I still love to dance," she hinted. "It's a shame to waste such music."

"I'm not wasting the music. I'm enjoying it very much." He smiled, ignoring her suggestion. "You didn't think we came for the food, did you?" he joked. "Not to change the subject or anything, but do you ever get hungry for some good old American fried chicken?"

"Say no more," she flipped, "or I won't be able to get down another mouthful of this stuff."

"It's better than army food."

"Prove it," she demanded, trimming a bit of greasy meat from the bone. It didn't even claim to be lamb. "At least they admit mutton's mutton."

"You know what army chow reminds me of?" he teased. "The co-op."

She did laugh, then, a good, hearty laugh, and he joined in as if pleased with his success. "I thought that would cheer you up."

"Right. When things get bad, you can always think of something worse. Remember when we got those turkeys cheap right after New Year's?"

"And for two weeks all we got delivered from Central Kitchen was turkey hash, turkey stew, turkey soup." Ron toyed with his own mutton chop. "We fellows organized a strike, remember? We refused to do any more central kitchen shifts until the cook came up with something besides turkey!"

"I sure remember that. You thought you were so smart. And we girls had to cover for you, or nobody would have gotten any hot meals."

"There's always peanut butter," Ron quoted, with a perfectly straight face, and they both exploded into laughter again.

"Wouldn't you love to see one of those half-gallon jars of it right now?" She choked through her laughter, "Oil on top and impenetrable goo at the bottom."

"Or just about anything else on a 'free snack' list."

Over a sticky pudding dessert, they traded memories of water fights, intra-house trophy thefts, bonfires before the big game. "The biggest crisis we faced was when Stanford stole the Ax," Ellen said wistfully.

"Not quite," Ron reminded her. "We were growing up, even then, and growing up is never easy." He reached for her hands across the table. "That's when our dreams split apart, yours and mine. That's when you drifted away from me."

"Was that how you saw it, Ron?"

"I know I'm the one who first put it into words, Ellen, but only after you made it clear you didn't want the same things from life that I did."

"What things? I never wanted the war, if that's what you mean?"

"How well I remember the way we fought over that peace committee." He did not mention that the peace committee she had been so dedicated to had totally collapsed the day Germany invaded Russia.

"Nice of you not to say 'I told you so,' when the Hitler-Stalin pact exploded," Ellen conceded. "So I was taken in. But that doesn't mean working for peace was wrong."

"Of course not. But you know it was more than that. Ellen, I was crazy about you, always had been, ever since you were in pigtails."

Ron's eyes met hers, and he looked down as he drew

171

his hands away. *Almost as if he were dropping a too-hot casserole*, she thought. It was a strange analogy. Her own hands turned cold.

"If you're finished with the pudding, maybe we'd better get back to the base," he said. "We fly again tomorrow."

They passed each other in the Officers' Club once or twice over the next couple of weeks. He waved; she smiled. *He is avoiding me*, Ellen was sure. *But why?* She took an empty seat near him at supper once. He was civil, but little more.

"Lovers' quarrel?" Cathy asked.

"I told you we aren't lovers," Ellen snapped.

"'The lady doth protest too much, methinks.'"

"Nonsense," Ellen retorted.

It was the third of June, a blustery Saturday with a furious storm approaching off the North Sea. The entire base was tense, alert, like a bowstring pulled tight, its arrow quivering at the point of release. All leaves had been cancelled.

"It can't be now," they assured each other. "Not in this weather."

The Flying Fortresses flew anyway, hoping to spot the right targets by radar. Ellen kept track, from the busy hospital, of the take-off of Ron's squadron, and of its return. Only three planes lost this time. His?

Another nurse handed her a message. Ron had called to tell her he was back and wanted to see her that evening. She went on about her duties, her step lighter, her face brighter.

They met at the mess hall door. The rain had turned her wavy hair into tight ringlets around her face. He fumbled for a handkerchief in the pocket of his leather flight jacket and wiped a raindrop from the tip of her nose.

They nibbled at the tough, flavorless roast beef, the lumpy mashed potatoes bitter with the taste of powdered milk, and the mushy, overcooked canned peas. Ron scarcely spoke.

"The condemned men ate a hearty meal," someone at the table joked. No one laughed.

"Do you mind a walk in the rain?" Ron asked, when Ellen laid her fork across her plate. "I know it's stormy, but there are so few places around here where we can be alone."

The rain had let up a little, but the evening sky was slate gray. "It's coming," Ron said. "Ellen, maybe this is silly. I'm not given to morbidity, but I just have this awful feeling that I have to talk to you, really talk to you—that there might not be another chance."

"You mustn't say that, Ron. You've made lots of runs. You have a guardian angel on your wing," she reminded him.

"I have had. But the invasion is coming, Ellen. Maybe sooner than we think."

"As soon as the weather clears, I imagine, but that should make things safer for you, if anything."

"Eventually—when we start moving inland." He took her hand as they jumped a small puddle in the path, and didn't let go. "But those first few days, weeks. Ellen, a lot of us aren't going to make it home."

"You will. You always do."

The rain had started again. Hurriedly, Ron drew her toward the little base chapel with its plain, white cross on top. "It's probably empty," he explained, "and it's certainly drier."

He gently pulled her down beside him on a back pew. He slipped out of the heavy flight jacket and put it around her damp shoulders.

"You're really afraid, aren't you?" she asked, puzzled by the change in him. "For the first time in your life, you're afraid. Is that why you wanted to see me tonight, Ron?"

He nodded. "I just have this gut feeling. I can't explain it, but this time I'm not sure I'll be coming back." He took her hands again. "Ellen, there are some things that need to be said between us. I don't know if I can make you understand, but I can't leave you again without trying."

"Best friends always understand," she reminded him.

"Best friends." He sighed deeply. "Ellen, it's always been more than that for me. Surely you know that. If only . . ." He looked away from her, up, toward the simple altar. "Ellen, if I don't come back . . . Maybe it isn't right, but I'm not ready to leave you."

He bit his lips, and Ellen thought she saw tears in his eyes. "Listen to me, please. Ellen, I don't want to die without . . ."

His grasp on her hands was so tight it hurt. And the pain reached the secret place in her heart she thought she had long ago sealed off. *It's just the war*, she warned herself. *The war and the uncertainty of everything but this moment.*

"Ellen, I had to break off with you back in the spring of 1940. God knows I didn't want to, but I had to. And when you gave me back my class ring—" He seemed to choke on the words. "The only mistake I made was not doing a cleaner job of leaving you—of putting you out of my life."

"Ron . . ." Ellen was confused. His pleading eyes, the way his hands gripped hers, his nearness in the darkening chapel all shouted the words she suddenly knew she wanted to hear, but his lips still spoke only of distance.

He looked around the little chapel, and she knew he was seeing all the symbols of the one he loved more than he could ever love her. His words confirmed her thoughts. "Ellen, I know I must never allow anyone to be more important to me than my God, no matter how much I care . . ." His voice dropped so she could scarcely hear the words. "And I do care, terribly."

"Ron, it's all right," she whispered, slipping even closer to him on the hard bench.

"But it isn't." He edged away from her. "That's just it, Ellen; I have to stop seeing you. If I do get through this war, it has to be over between us, really over."

He didn't mean it, she knew. Not now, when they were suddenly so close, closer than they had ever been. She rested her head on his shoulder.

"Ellen." It was almost a groan. "Oh, Ellen, I had no right to let this happen."

"But what has happened except that we've found our way back to each other at last?"

"Ellen, I should never have brought you here tonight.

I told myself it would be just one last heart-to-heart talk between friends, but I should have known better."

"Not the last. Nothing's going to happen to you." She brushed back a stray lock of hair from his forehead. "Ron, we'll make a new start."

He cupped her face in his hands. "Ellen, I'm afraid. I brought you here tonight because I wanted to be with you one more time. Because I wanted to look at you, and touch you, and, God forgive me, love you, just once."

"Ron, we love each other. We want each other. Is that so wrong?" But she knew that for him it was wrong.

"I do love you." He'd said the words she wanted to hear, but his voice was strangely distant.

She wanted his arms around her, his lips on hers, but he pushed her away instead. His hands dropped, and she realized his fists were clenched. "Ellen, I'd better take you back to your quarters."

"Not now. Not now, please. Not now, when we are so near to making a new start. I'll try, Ron. I'll try to be what you need."

"We've tried before, Ellen. It worked, sort of, when we were thousands of miles apart." His hands were rough as he zipped her into his warm jacket. "But it isn't working. I haven't the strength to be only your friend. I can't trust myself. If I can't have you as my wife, and I can't, darling, then God help me, I dare not, I must not see you at all."

"But . . ."

His voice was husky with desire. "Ellen, it's got to end, one way or another."

She nearly had to run to keep up with his determined stride as they walked back to the nurses' Quonset hut. He left her at the door. And he didn't look back as he headed toward his own quarters.

Chapter Eighteen

Y ou're going to church?"
Cathy was incredulous.
"You haven't been to a church service since I've known
you."

Ellen shrugged as she settled her pert, peaked overseas
cap into her soft waves. "I'm not sure why I'm going,
Cathy. But, well, something big is about to happen.
Maybe I figure our men need all the help they can get.
Anyhow, it just seems like the right thing to do."

Ron's words and his changed attitude had frightened
her more than she was willing to admit even to herself.
What if he doesn't come back next time? She tried not to
think about it as she walked toward the little base chapel.
How could I ever go on without him?

But we can never go back to being just friends, she knew.
Her blood raced as she recalled the ache in his voice, and
the longing in his eyes, and, yes, the heat of his touch on
her hands, her shoulders, her face. *He wanted me.* Suddenly she understood the bewildering shifts of mood, the

long periods of cool avoidance interrupted by jarring moments of closeness. *He's never stopped loving me, but he has that crazy notion that loving me is a sin, just because I'm not his kind of Christian.*

Hundreds of young couples had found secret places in the past few days, she knew, snatching at a few moments of intimacy before the invasion that might separate them forever. *And Ron wanted me.* A strange melancholy touched her. *Oh, please don't let it be too late.*

She slipped into a crowded pew. *We were always destined for each other*, she realized. *He knows it, and now I know it. Maybe there's still time.* She looked around, but his tawny head and tanned face were nowhere to be seen. *Oh, please don't let it be too late*, she prayed to the God she said she didn't believe in.

She tried to listen to the sermon. *Maybe it will help me to understand Ron*, she hoped.

The chaplain knew what they all knew, that the long-anticipated invasion was near. Like each one of them, he avoided, for security reasons, any public mention of pervading private thoughts. He read from Psalm 27: "Though war may rise against me, in this will I be confident. . . . For in the time of trouble He shall hide me in His pavilion."

That is what Ron has always been, she thought, *a David, sure that God will protect him. If he ever lost that* . . . She recalled the moments in this same chapel two nights before. *If Ron betrayed his God he would be betraying himself. And he almost had*, she realized. *Is that why he was afraid? Does he really think it's a sin for a man to want a woman?*

". . . My heart said to You, "Your face, LORD, I will

seek," the chaplain read. *It's a sin to want anything more than you want God. At least it is to Ron.* She was not even trying to listen to the sermon any more. *He's up there right now, probably, fighting for his life. And he loves me. And he believes that loving me makes him unfaithful to his God.*

She still did not understand. A jealous God didn't fit her picture of what a god should be. *But if you are up there, God, you must know that Ron does love you, and he loves you more than he loves me. So please don't punish him just for loving me too. And please, please don't punish him for my unbelief.*

Ron was flying that Sunday despite a steady downpour and high winds off the North Sea. The squadron returned, but there was no word from him. Ellen was on duty that night; many of the planes that returned were back in the air in just a few hours, and she supposed his was among them.

Monday the storm was even worse. "No invasion this week," they reassured each other as the winds howled and the rain drummed on the tin roof of the hospital.

But Monday night they heard a disarming lull in the storm. And they heard the uninterrupted drone of planes overhead, and the hum of trucks on the slick roads. Nothing was said. Everything was felt. The bulletin board carried a strange message at midnight: ALL MEDICAL PERSONNEL REPORT FOR DUTY AT 0600. NO EXCEPTIONS!

Ellen was certain that no one who lived through that cold, overcast Tuesday, June 6, 1944, would ever forget it. By 5:00 A.M., when she gave up trying to sleep, there was no more need for secrecy. Planes did not take off or land in isolated groups. Their movement was continuous. And so, all too soon, was the flow of stretchers into the base hospital.

The men who were able to speak told horror stories. They had flown in low over the Normandy coast, so low they could see the men pouring out of the clumsy-looking landing craft into the cold, choppy waves. "The men were so loaded down with equipment they couldn't swim, nurse. If somebody goofed and dumped them too far off-shore, they never made it to the beach."

"I took out a couple of pillboxes, anyhow," a tail-gunner bragged. "That was a few less bullets to mow our guys down." He winced as Ellen poured iodine into the gaping hole in his thigh. "Gad, it was awful. The second wave had to walk over the bodies of the first. The slaughter! I'm sure glad I wasn't down on that beach."

Ellen's hand trembled as she bandaged the ugly wound. "But we'll lick 'em, nurse," he vowed. "We'll hold on to that beach, and we'll send those Nazis running all the way back to Berlin with their tails between their legs."

The frothy waves of the English Channel were red with blood they said. Still, by evening the American, Canadian, and English infantry and marines had tight toeholds on places they called Utah Beach, Gold, Sword, and Juno.

"It was worst at Omaha Beach," a bombardier with a shattered elbow told Ellen. "I got a pretty good view before I laid my eggs on the railyards at Le Havre. We've got to keep those trains from getting through. Our engineers are putting floating docks together, and you wouldn't believe the ships. We've got everything that can float loaded down with supplies," he told her. "But all Hitler's got to do is put his stuff on those trains."

"Yeah, you worry about the German trains," a downy-faced boy interrupted. His tawny hair was matted with black, clotted blood from a scalp wound. He reminded her of Ron, the Ron she had known back in Soledad. "Us fighter pilots are going to win the war. We're what's keeping the Luftwaffe from touching those supply ships."

Ellen had no idea what time it was when Major Schaeffer touched her shoulder. "Better take a break, Lt. Hanlon. Get some sleep, and be back by 0600 tomorrow."

Ellen stumbled back to the nurses' quarters, surprised to see a black night sky. Stars twinkled between the regathering storm clouds.

It was impossible to keep the days straight. Ellen's shifts began whenever the major decided she had had enough sleep, and ended when she could no longer see what she was doing. If the sky were dark, it was night; if it were gray or, by some chance, the sun peeped through, then it was day. Which night? Which day? "I think it's still June," Ellen muttered once or twice. If she needed to know for sure, she checked the most recent entry on a patient's chart.

The Friday evening with Ron, the assurance that he still loved her faded into the dim past, the time before D-Day. Once in a while, as she sank, exhausted, into her bed, she would remember that she had not heard from him since Friday. *Under the circumstances*, she assured herself, *no news is good news. Surely if anything has happened to him, someone would have let me know.*

The posted orders on the hospital bulletin board told her she was taking a flight of evacuees to Washington on the eleventh. She had to think for a minute. Yes, that would be day after tomorrow. She headed toward the mess hall, and looked around, hoping to find Ron there. It was Jim Roberts who called to her.

He was tired too. A black stubble darkened his cheeks; a black shadow clouded his eyes. "Maybe the worst is over," he sighed, as she sat down beside him. "Tough about Ron, isn't it?"

She gulped, wordless.

"Hey, I'm sorry," he mumbled awkwardly. "I just assumed you'd heard. I'm awfully sorry."

She heard, again, Ron's words that Saturday night less than a week ago. *"This time I might not come back."* She could not ask the question. She was too afraid of Jim's answer. "It's been almost a week since I heard from him," she said, her voice trembling.

Jim hesitated.

He's trying to break it to me gently, she knew. Why doesn't he just get it over with? "When?" she asked.

"Sunday. We saw chutes, Ellen. Some of them got out in time."

She tried to listen, to follow his disjointed report. *Ron went down. Sunday. Oh, God, how could you fail him when he trusted you so?*

"Ellen, did you hear me? I said there were chutes. The plane exploded, but some of them got out in time. We're talking about Lucky Stephens, Ellen. I'm sure he's sitting in some French farmer's kitchen right now drinking a glass of champagne—no, not that, not him." Jim forced a smile. "But he's all right. I'm sure he just got into France a little ahead of the rest of us."

"Were you there, Jim? Tell me exactly what happened."

He fumbled with his fork. "I wasn't really close, Ellen. We had a mission over Calais. Calais," he repeated flatly. "We didn't know it then, of course, but Calais was just a feint, to make them think that was where we were going to land." He sighed. "Ironic, isn't it, that Lucky went down on a phony mission. But at least the trick seems to have worked. The Germans are confused."

"Jim," she pleaded. "Jim, how did it happen?"

"The flak was bad, as usual. But there were only a few German fighters. The pilot on Ron's wing said it must have been the flak. Ron lost control. He dropped out of formation, and the Messerschmitts were after him like buzzards."

Ellen shuddered as a horrible picture crossed her mind—Ron's plane, and him in it, crashing into the French countryside, a mass of flame. "No!" she moaned.

"Ellen, we counted chutes. Before she blew up we counted four chutes. You mustn't give up hope."

A week ago she would have been certain he was safe, but now Ron's strange premonition lay heavy on her heart. *Could he really be gone? Could that God of his be real and vengeful? Could God have let him die rather than let us love each other?* she wondered as she checked her flight bag the next afternoon.

Someone knocked. She opened the door and was surprised to see the base chaplain, a small package in his hand. He shifted uneasily. "Ellen Hanlon?" he asked. "I'm sorry I haven't had a chance to get to know you." He glanced at the package. "I knew Ron, though. I'm so sorry he's missing. Of course, we must not give up hope that he is safe, but if not, surely we have the assurance that he . . ."

"That thought was a comfort to him, I know," Ellen interrupted sharply, unwilling to listen to the chaplain's platitudes.

She reached out, and he handed her the package. "We found this among the things we are sending to his mother. It was addressed to you."

His Bible. She laid it on her bed. *The most precious thing he owned, and he wanted it to be precious to me too. A small book lay with it. The Screwtape Letters.* The book was a favorite of Ron's, written recently by a don at Cambridge. "You'd appreciate the wit," Ron had told her. "God and man from the devil's viewpoint."

She picked up the letter, addressed in his familiar hand and opened it.

"My dearest Ellen," he began.

I've never done this before, but as I told you in the chapel, I have this strange feeling that I might not get back tomorrow. Ellen, did I tell you last night? Have I ever, ever, told you that I love you? I guess I always have, and I suspect I always will.

If you are reading this, it means my premonition was right. Blame God, if you must, but if you blame him, at least that will prove you do believe in him. And you must see that if we believe in him, we really must choose either to serve him or to fight him. There was never a choice for me. And I knew I could never serve him as he deserved with an unbelieving wife by my side.

That has been my cross, Ellen. Seeing you, loving you, being tempted by you. The Bible says that he will never let us be tempted beyond our ability to resist, so, if God chooses to take me to be with him, perhaps that is another example of his mercy. At least the pain of seeing you and not having you would be ended.

If I am taken to him, I know I will be at peace. But I think, even then, I will miss you. I guess that's why I'm leaving you my Bible. Perhaps because it was mine you will choose to read it with new eyes. As for Screwtape I'm not sure. But God seems to be telling me you should read it.

I love you, Ellen.

Your best friend, always,
Ron

She had been trying to cry ever since Jim's news. Now the tears came, flooding, burning, blinding. *There were parachutes*, she told herself. But the tears kept coming.

There was another knock on the door, quick and sharp. "Ellen, they're waiting for you to supervise the loading for your flight."

She shook away her grief, bathed her swollen face, and started to zip the flight bag. She didn't know why, but she picked up the little book and dropped it into the bag as she went out the door and headed across the teeming airfield.

Chapter Nineteen

The twin motors of the Skytrain drummed in her ears. She should have been sleeping. She had had only a two-hour lay-over between seeing her wounded patients into the waiting ambulances and boarding the C-47 headed back to England. But whenever she closed her eyes she saw Ron's Flying Fortress, a falling ball of fire, and his face amidst the flame.

She wanted to cling to the hope that one of the parachutes had been his, but there had been only four. And Ron would never have bailed out before his crew. *The plane suddenly went out of control, Jim had said, though it didn't appear to be badly damaged. It left formation.* That was unthinkable, unless . . . *Unless Ron, himself, had been hit and unable to pilot the bomber.*

She thought of the little book in her flight bag. *Why bother to read it now? Maybe if Ron were here.* She brushed away hopeless tears. *But it doesn't matter any more. It's too late.*

She wriggled in the uncomfortable jump seat and closed her eyes. But she still saw his face, still, unbelievably, with its carefree grin, still circled with fire. *Where was his God then?*

Maybe there just isn't any God, she thought. But Ellen had never been able to completely accept that conclusion. There was too much evidence—the beauty of the universe, the precise order of creation, the spirit of man.

Is God weak, then? He doesn't seem to be able to keep the human race from killing itself. He couldn't even protect Ron in the end.

Cruel? Does God just play with us, cat-and-mouse fashion? Is life a game played for God's amusement? And then when he's tired of playing at last, he comes in for the kill?

If that were true, she reasoned, *the only rational thing to do would be to end the game—kill each other, kill ourselves, rob the cat of its pleasure.* It made a cruel sort of sense to Ellen, *a diabolical sense.* The word was a strange one to come to her mind, she thought.

But if God is that evil, her logical mind argued, *then where did humans ever get the idea of good anyhow? Oh why can't I just believe, like Marianne, like Ron? Oh, Ron, I need your God. I want to believe, and now you're not here to help me.*

But maybe Ron was there, in a way. She dug into the bag and took out the little book. Idly she flipped the pages. It was silly—just a series of letters from one devil to another. *But it was important to Ron.*

A page caught her eye. He had underlined a passage.

He wants them to learn to walk and must therefore take

away His hand; and if only the will to walk is really
there He is pleased even with their stumbles.

*A cat, letting the mouse go for the joy of catching it again?
Or a father, letting his toddler fall for the joy of seeing the child
stand up again and walk?*
When at long last she dozed, she saw Ron's face again,
still smiling, untouched by the flame.

Ellen read the little book from cover to cover. Despite
her grief, she caught herself smiling at the subtle irony of
C. S. Lewis's fantasy.

He cannot ravish. He can only woo. For His ignoble
idea is to eat the cake and have it; the creatures are to
be one with Him, but yet themselves; merely to cancel
them, or assimilate them, will not serve.

Free will, she murmured. *That was what Marianne was
always talking about. If we only loved him and served him
because we had no choice, that would be meaningless. He
wants our love given freely, by our choice.*
All right, she conceded. *So I believe you exist; I believe
you are good; I even believe, maybe, for the sake of argument
. . .* She wondered, briefly, at her audacity in arguing with
God, but who else was there to help her reason it out?
Marianne was in California and Ron? Ron, she confessed
as the ache began again in her heart, was probably dead.
So she argued with God. *Even if I believe that I should
love you, how can I force love? You want me to choose to love*

you, but love isn't a choice. It's a feeling, a reaction, a response.

But she would try, she resolved. She would see the chaplain, she promised herself, as the plane dropped onto the green English earth. But first, she checked her orders. She found she had only ten hours before her next flight. *Ten hours to get a good meal, some sleep, and be back in the air!*

She checked with base headquarters. "No," the clerk told her, trying to soften the officious snap of his hurried answer. "Nothing new on Major Stephens. Sorry, ma'am, but all I have is that he's officially Missing in Action."

She slept, too exhausted even for her nightmares. She put on her last fresh uniform, went through the motions of breakfast, and reported for her flight. No litters were waiting on the tarmac for loading. "Is there some mistake? Am I early?" she asked the pilot who was making the standard pre-flight inspection of the C-47.

"You the flight nurse? You're right on time. Climb aboard."

"But where are my patients?"

"Oh, didn't you know? We're headed for France. The landing forces have captured an airstrip near Ste. Mère Église, and we're picking up a load from a field hospital."

This was what she had been trained for, the challenge she had been so eager for when she volunteered for flight duty. But she was totally unprepared for the chaos of the sagging tent, hastily pitched alongside the bomb-cratered runway, or the overflow of litters strewn in disarray outside the tent.

Ellen soon realized the disarray was only apparent. She picked her way among groaning men. These were the less-seriously injured, her trained eye told her, despite the bloody bandages and agonized appeals for help. A nurse worked a few yards away. At least Ellen assumed she was a nurse, though instead of a uniform she wore an ill-fitting camouflage coverall, and her hair was tucked into a too-large helmet.

The busy nurse knelt to inspect a wound or offer a word of comfort, then stood, waving directions to the waiting corpsmen. This one inside, to emergency surgery; that one to a quiet spot on the edge of the field where a chaplain offered comfort to those beyond help. Most, though, were just moved to other spots in the sunny field, out of the way, to be tended as time allowed.

Ellen felt terribly out of place in her starched white uniform. But the other nurse called to her. "Your patients are that group to your right. We've got them stabilized, but they need more care than we can give them here."

Fourteen men at her feet, and three more groups of fourteen stretching beyond, waiting for the next flights. It was chaos, she thought, but there was hope amid the chaos, and she was part of that hope.

Amid the groans, corpsmen attached bottles of blood plasma to poles fastened to the litters and checked I.V. needles. Most of the men lay quietly, with closed eyes, sedated. A few were awake.

"Nurse, you got a cigarette?" Ellen checked his chart, lit a cigarette, and placed it between the bandages that covered his face.

"A little water, nurse?" another soldier asked. She held a tin cup to his cracked lips.

"What's your phone number?" She laughed, and assured him she would be his first date back in England.

On each blanket was a crisp summary of diagnosis and treatment given so far. Ellen's eyes scanned them, absorbing the essentials virtually by osmosis, as the litters were loaded into the waiting plane.

She looked at her watch as they took off. Less than an hour on the ground. Another two, and they would be unloading in southern England. She began her rounds, checking each man's vital signs, dressings, and morale.

Her questions were still with her. Though God was more real to her than he had ever been before, she still thought of him as Ron's God, not hers. *I believe in him,* she told herself, *but how can I know him, like Ron did? How can I love him? How can I become his child?*

The answers would have to wait. *If God expects anything more from me right now than what I'm doing, that's tough. I'm a nurse, and these men need me.*

She flew back and forth to France almost every day, and sometimes twice in one day. There were always too many wounded, and always she looked at each face, somehow hoping that Ron was still alive and had managed to get through the German lines.

She did talk to the chaplain once or twice, but all he told her was that she must put her trust in Jesus. "Jesus is our way to God."

But how? Who is, was, Jesus? Wasn't he God, himself? But Jesus died. She wanted to understand. *How can I believe what I can't understand?* She tried reading Ron's

194

Bible during her few spare moments. At least while she was reading his Bible she could feel for a little while that Ron was still with her.

Then she met Tony. It was on a long flight back to the States. Tony had been blinded by an exploding mine at Omaha Beach, and nothing more could be done for him, so he was going home to New York City. "Nurse," he asked her as she sponged his disfigured face, "if you have time, could you read to me for a while?"

"Sure, as soon as I check out your buddies."

She finished the hourly rounds of the wounded men, and went back to Tony. "What do you want me to read?" she asked.

"My Bible, please, ma'am. It's there, in my duffel bag."

She reached for the bag at the foot of his litter, and found the little steel-covered New Testament the Salvation Army gave to soldiers. "Anything in particular?"

"Philippians," he told her without hesitation. "The joy book."

Philippians. Paul's epistles. She leafed past the Gospels and the Acts. "I'll have it in just a second," she assured the sightless young man. "Why do you call it the 'joy' book?"

"Why, nurse, that's what it's all about—how we can have joy from God no matter what happens. Read me chapter four, slowly. I'm trying to memorize it."

"'Rejoice in the Lord always,'" she read. The scarred face on the pillow was impassive, but Ellen sensed that the man behind the ruined skin and muscle was not impassive. "'Be anxious for nothing, but in everything by prayer and supplication, with thanksgiving, let your requests be made known to God; and the peace of God, which surpasses all understanding, will guard your hearts and minds through Christ Jesus.'"

The words were familiar even to Ellen, but how could this man find comfort in them, this man whom God had let be so terribly hurt?

"I couldn't live without that, Nurse. How do people survive who don't know him?"

"How? Can I ask you a question, Tony?"

"How can I thank him, when he hasn't healed my eyes? That's what everybody asks me."

But that was not the question Ellen wanted to ask. "I grew up going to Sunday school, and I know God didn't promise healing or wealth or any of those things. But he did promise peace, and he's obviously given you that. How can I have that peace, Tony?"

He groped for her hand; his misshapen lips formed what she knew was a soundless prayer. "Nurse . . ."

"Ellen," she interrupted softly.

"Ellen," he murmured. "He gives it, no strings. But you have to ask. You have to let go and admit you need him. You said you went to Sunday school, so you must know it's sin that keeps us from him."

She nodded, then realized that was no answer for the blind Tony. "But what really is sin?" she asked. "I don't . . . I'm not . . . Tony, I try to be good."

"Flip that Bible to Matthew 22, verse 37. What does it say?"

"'You shall love the LORD your God with all your heart, with all your soul, and with all your mind.'"

"Most people only read what comes after that,

about loving our neighbor," Tony said. "But what did Jesus say?"

"To love him first."

"That's the real rub, isn't it? I don't love him like that; you don't; nobody does."

"Ron did." She said it so softly she was sure he couldn't have heard.

"Nobody," he insisted. "Even if some do come closer than others." He paused. He seemed to be praying again. "Who was Ron, or shouldn't I ask?"

"Someone you had a lot in common with," she told Tony. "Someone who didn't have a lot in common with me. He loved me, but he loved God more. So he left me behind and went off to do his duty to God and country. He was shot down over Calais."

"You loved him, too, didn't you?"

"More than I knew, until it was too late. But it wouldn't have mattered. He never would have married me. He never would have married anyone who didn't put Jesus first."

"How do you feel about God now, Ellen? Do you want to believe there is no God, because he didn't protect Ron? You could hate God, I guess, for taking your love away from you. But you said you wanted God's peace."

"And I do. I can't think about Ron without thinking about his strength and his hope. He had a premonition. He left a letter. He thought maybe God would take him so that he wouldn't have to . . ." It was a private thought, but she knew she could trust this blind stranger. "He looked on death as an end to a temptation he was struggling against. He thought he was going to die, and he didn't want to. But he was sure that whatever God did was right."

"'Though I walk through the valley of the shadow of death,'" Tony whispered.

"That's what I want, Tony, that sense that the God who has my life in his hands loves me enough, and has power enough, to take care of me. Because I can't take care of myself."

"If that's what you really want, then you're almost there."

"I know the words," she told him. "I know that the Bible says I am a sinner, and no matter how good I might think I've been, I've certainly failed him. But I have to have faith, and I don't."

"What does Ephesians 2:8 and 9 say?"

She still held Tony's Bible, but she remembered those verses from Sunday school. "By grace you have been saved through faith, and that not of yourselves; it is the gift of God . . ."

"It is the gift of God—faith. We know he doesn't always give us what we ask for, but this is one prayer he never delays answering."

He paused, and she knew he was praying again. "You must be sure, Ellen, that you really want that kind of faith. God is a loving Father, and he'll never leave you, but he will discipline you. Faith is a gift, but it has to be exercised. Just give yourself to him, Ellen. You won't always under-stand. You won't always be happy, but once you take that gift of faith, the other gifts—love, joy, peace—will all come to you the same way, free for the asking."

Words from a long-forgotten Sunday school lesson

came to her mind. "Lord, I believe," she said softly. "Help thou mine unbelief. Give me the gift of faith, Lord," she prayed. "I can't find it on my own; I don't deserve it, and I never could. But I want to trust you, like Ron did. I want to serve you, like he did, and like Marianne does. I want to be your child, and to live for you."

The peace came in like a flood. If Ron were in heaven, how wonderful, she knew, for him. She still missed him terribly, but she was no longer alone.

Her warm tears fell on Tony's cool hand. She daubed away the tears and took up the duty at hand. But when she had again made the circuit of the litters on the plane, she went back to Tony. At first she thought he was asleep, and she started to step away. "Is that you, Ellen?" he whispered.

"I thought you were sleeping," she told him. "You should be. You need your rest."

"Not as much as I needed our talk."

"You needed it?" she questioned. "You just led me to Jesus. You helped me to find the purpose and meaning of my existence and you say *you* needed our talk?"

"Yes. When they put me on this plane I wanted to die. I have pleaded with God for death, and even thought about taking my own life. Ellen, I love him, and I never wanted anything, as far back as I can remember, but to be a preacher. Then my buddy stepped on that mine, and everything blew up in my face. Not just the landmine. The dream. A blind preacher? I thought God must have rejected me. I thought I wasn't good enough to serve him, or he would have prevented my blindness."

199

"You can see far better than I, Tony," Elllen protested. "Your sight is gone, but you know the way to the light."

"That's what I mean," he said softly. "The Lord used you, Ellen, to show me that I can still serve him."

Chapter Twenty

You haven't had any news about Ron, have you?" Cathy asked, as they walked from the hospital back to their quarters a few days after Ellen's return from New York.

"No, I haven't, Cathy. His name still hasn't turned up on the POW lists." She had hoped, she admitted to herself, that God would reward her confession of faith with good news. *But that kind of hope is more like one of Screwtape's lies than the hope we have in Christ,* she had warned herself, even as she had gone to base headquarters to ask for news.

"Of course that doesn't mean he hasn't been picked up by the French Resistance," she told Cathy. "Getting out of the Calais area right now would not be easy."

"Sure," Cathy assured her. "But I thought maybe you had heard something definite. You seem so much happier. No, not happier, I guess, but content, since you got back from the U.S."

"I am, Cathy. I didn't realize it showed."

Cathy nodded. "You're not so preoccupied. And you haven't bitten anyone's head off since you got back, either."

"Have I been that hard to live with?"

"Ellen, we understood. We all knew about Ron, and for all your protestations about being just friends, well, let's just say I'd give the world for a friend like that."

Ellen's eyes watered. "I miss him, Cathy, more than I ever thought I would, more than I can put into words. And I think I miss him even more now than I did at first." *How do I explain why?* Ellen wondered. *I've always pooh-poohed religion to her.*

"Something did happen on the flight home, Cathy, something I never thought would happen to me. I'd love to be able to tell Ron about it. It would make him so happy. To put it simply, I have found peace. I had been reading the book Ron left and his Bible. I wanted what he had, the peace, the assurance."

"But you said you couldn't believe all that."

"I couldn't. Cathy, there was a kid on the plane. A mine had blown up in his face. He was blind, but he could see so much better than I could. He had lost his sight and he was terribly disfigured, but he still had that same peace Ron had. And he showed me how to find it for myself."

Cathy shook her head. "I don't understand it, but I know you've changed. I'm happy for you. But I sure never expected to hear you talking like this." Cathy pushed the door open, and they walked into the bare little room they shared. "You always said it didn't make sense. Well, it still doesn't to me."

"I had it all wrong. I thought I had to understand first, and then maybe I could believe," Ellen explained. "But we can't understand God's message by ourselves. We have to believe, first. And only God can give us faith, Cathy. I guess it isn't up to us to figure out why. If we could, we'd be gods too. He wants us to have faith, each and every one of us, but we have to ask for it. If faith were just something we were born with, we'd be nothing but puppets. But God wants individuals. He can only be satisfied if we love him, and serve him, of our own free will."

They sat opposite each other on their narrow army cots. "We've both had that preached to us all our lives," Cathy protested. "Last week that message was as incomprehensible to you as it is to me."

"But I tried believing, Cathy. I was so alone. I couldn't go to Ron and borrow strength from his faith. I needed, desperately, what he had had. And there, on that C-47 full of half-men, in a physical sense, I asked God to make me whole, spiritually. I asked him to give me the faith, and he did."

It was September already. In France, the troops seemed to be bogged down just a few miles inland. Cherbourg had fallen, and, finally, Caen. But the steamroller advance to the Rhine they had hoped for was met with resistance they had thought beyond the strength of the weary German Army. Calais—Ellen still thought often of Calais. The German stronghold had simply been bypassed.

Ellen had been to church that morning. She never missed a service now unless she was on duty. *The same old 'cart before the horse' syndrome,* she reflected. *Before I trusted Jesus, I went, sometimes, but it all sounded so foolish. Now, I find new blessings in every service.*

She had tried to explain the change in her life to her friends. She wrote about it to Kim, and talked to Cathy, the other nurses, Jim. She smiled to herself. Jim always listened, as she suspected he had listened to Ron, with that amused, indulgent smile on his face. *Well, why should he be different?* She prayed for him, as she knew Ron had prayed for him, *as Ron had prayed for me,* she thought with a heavy heart.

The war had become routine, if blood, and pain, and death could possibly be called routine. For the Air Force, the worst was over, but that did not mean planes stopped returning to base battle-scarred, carrying battle-scarred men.

Ellen's evac flights went deeper into France each week; the field hospitals followed the battle lines that advanced steadily, but frustratingly slowly. Each new site looked pretty much the same as the one before—khaki tent topped with a bright red cross, men on litters waiting their turns outside, a field of white crosses marking fresh graves a few hundred yards away.

There were too few nurses qualified to take charge on the desperate flights back from France. Ellen did the work she was trained to do with a heavy heart, but she knew, terrible as it was, that she was relieving some of the terror.

On Wednesday, she was off duty, and wrote to Marianne. It was such a joy, now, to share each of God's little miracles with her mother. Ellen scarcely looked up as she heard the familiar sputter of a Flying Fortress limping home.

The phone rang, and she reached for it. "Ellen?" It was the base chaplain. "Ellen, one of the men who just came in has asked to see you. Could you come over to the hospital right away?"

"Who?"

"It's Jim Roberts. He's got a bad belly wound. They're taking him to surgery, and the doctor says it will be touch and go. That's why they called me. But he wants to see you."

"I'm on my way."

She grabbed the well-worn Bible, the one that had been Ron's. She prayed as she ran. She found Jim on a gurney outside surgery. She knew instantly that his condition was critical. "Jim, it's Ellen. I'm here."

He lifted his hand an inch or so from the blanket, but it fell again. She picked it up in hers. "I know it's bad," she told him, "but you'll be fine once the surgery is over."

"Ellen," he whispered, "I'm scared."

"Nonsense," she lied. "They just have to do a little snipping and stitching. You'll probably be on my next trip back to the States."

His head moved feebly. "Taking a longer trip than that. Last trip." He had to gather strength before he could say more. "Ellen, I'm dying, and I'm afraid."

"Jim, I'm not much of a liar. It's bad. But you're strong. You have to fight back."

"Too late." His hand trembled. "Ellen, I laughed." He coughed, weakly, and his mouth twisted in pain. "I laughed at God, and now I'm afraid to face him."

"You don't have to be, you know." *Oh, God, give me the words,* she prayed. "God loves you," she said softly.

"Does he?"

"'God so loved the world,'" she began, but Jim was trying to speak again, and she bent low over him to hear the words.

"You have to believe, Ellen. I didn't."

"Then why are you afraid?" She forced a smile. "You must believe, or you wouldn't be so afraid. Jim, if you believe . . ."

"I've been a heel, Ellen. I've ridiculed anything that smacked of religion." The confession seemed to exhaust him.

"So did I, for years. God is patient."

"Never thought much of death-bed conversions."

A corpsman came out of the operating room "We're just about ready for him, Lieutenant."

She leaned closer. "Jim, do you remember the story of the thief on the cross? Do you remember what Jesus told him?"

His eyes were closed, but his lips opened, mouthing the words he had learned in Sunday school and nearly forgotten. "Today you will be with Me in Paradise."

She sat in the hall and prayed as the surgeon worked inside. God could answer yes, but he didn't always. *It's like with Ron,* she sensed. *I want so much for him to be alive, and I want so much for Jim to live. But whatever happens, I will not let go of the faith God has given me.* "Thy will be done," she concluded.

The door opened, and the grim-faced surgeon came

out. "We did all we could. The internal damage was just too great."

Ellen's eyes filled with hot tears. She had prepared herself for bad news, but it still hurt. Jim's soul had been saved, and for that she thanked God. But she would miss him.

Ellen went back to her room and added the sad news in her letter to Marianne. Then she took another flimsy sheet of air-mail paper from its packet. She had been meaning to write to Mrs. Stephens for weeks, but what could she say?

Dear Mrs. Stephens,

You must have known how much Ron and I have meant to each other. Even though we broke up in college, we've always remained good friends, and the few weeks we had together here in England were very precious.

I can't tell him, now, how much he meant to me, but I want you, at least, to know that Ron's prayers have been answered. The memory of his words, and his godly life have borne their fruit, and I now trust Jesus as my Lord and Savior.

Mrs. Stephens, if God in his goodness should bring Ron back to us, that would be a joy beyond imagining, but if not, at least your son's life has had meaning. I praise God daily for the privilege of having known Ron and, yes, having loved him.

We must not give up the hope that Ron is still alive in France, but we know that if he isn't, he is alive forever with Jesus.

She signed the letter, sealed it, picked up the two envelopes and started out to mail them. On the way back she met the chaplain. "Jim is gone," she told him, "but he is with the Lord."

Chapter 21

The next Red Cross list of prisoners of war included two of Ron's crewmen. Happy as she was for those two and their families, she could not help remembering that only two other parachutes had been seen, and there were eight other crewmen. *One chance in four, by simple mathematics. Less, knowing Ron's selflessness.* Her new faith didn't fail her as she grieved, prayed for strength, and kept on working.

The flights to France were exhausting, but satisfying too. Ellen knew she was needed; God was using her. There were crises, and she knew how to respond. Sometimes neither her skill nor her prayers brought visible success. But sometimes men who might have died before they reached England's hospitals survived. And sometimes a man wounded beyond her healing skills heard words of hope, and died with Jesus' name on his lips.

Trips back to the United States were respites. The

men seldom required intensive care, and Germany was too busy in France and Russia to present much danger over the Atlantic. In late September, after a flight to Boston, Ellen took a few days leave. There was not time to fly home to California; but Kim had just finished her nurses' training in upstate New York, and together they spent a few days in Vermont.

Kim was quieter now, and Ellen missed the little tornado that used to hover over her friend. "You've changed, Kim," she said, as they settled into a little tourist cabin in the woods. "It was bad, wasn't it, in the camp?"

"It was okay. Really it was." Kim looked out the window at the full moon peeking through the trees.

"Well, it wasn't as bad as it might have been. If the stories are true, the Japanese army is brutal to its prisoners of war. We were prisoners, too, but we had plenty to eat, and the food was even pretty good once we got organized and started doing our own cooking.

"We managed to fix up the barracks," she went on. "And some of the older people even built little Japanese gardens with the stones and the desert plants. The government set up a clinic, and Ken and I both worked there. We had enough teachers to get schools set up for the kids."

"But you were still prisoners." Ellen slipped an arm around Kim's slender waist.

Kim nodded. "You can't know what it was like. Inside, we had a community and community structure. But then there was the barbed wire, and, outside, the desert. Ellen, my time there is over; it's over for most of us. Only the ones who couldn't find a place to go are still in the camps.

The Supreme Court is going to hear a test case soon, and then maybe everyone will be released."

"Your parents?"

"They're still at Manzanar. It's harder for the Issei to get permission to leave. Ken is doing fine, though. He got a residency in obstetrics at Ford Hospital in Detroit."

"Good for him. He wrote to me, you know, before he was married. I was so happy for him."

"And you?" Kim queried. "Your letters, well, sometimes it's hard to write about things like that, but you did find your way back, too, didn't you? Back to Ron. And then . . ."

"There's been no word, Kim. Maybe it was too late for us."

As Ellen prepared for bed, her eyes burned, and she let the tears slip down her cheeks. Kim sat beside her on the edge of the four-poster bed, but Ellen took Ron's Bible out of her overnight bag. "I'm fine, Kim." She wiped away the tears and opened the book. "I'm not alone any more."

Ellen's leave ended, and she was glad, in a way, to be getting back to her work. *I told Kim the truth*, she told herself. *I'm not alone*. Still, she was less lonely when she was busy.

As the plane neared England, she pictured again the glowing red and gold of the maples and birch on the Vermont hillsides and the prim white-steepled churches on the village greens in each little valley. *I wish I could share it with Ron*, she thought sadly.

Looking down as the Skytrain made its final approach, she compared the old England and the new. *As different*, she realized, *as the old Ellen and the new.*

As her plane hit, bounced, and slowed to a stop, she noticed an Air Force officer at the edge of the runway. He leaned heavily on a cane, and his uniform hung loosely on shoulders that were too broad for his thin torso. Although one leg dragged stiffly, he was suddenly almost running toward the plane.

Ellen's heartbeat quickened, but she refused the crazy hope she felt. *There are thousands of stocky, tawny-haired Air Force officers in England,* she told herself. She tried to sit patiently until the plane stopped. She picked up her flight bag and tried to be casual as she made her way to the exit and down the steep ladder. The man at the foot of the ladder had dropped his cane and stood waiting, arms open.

She dropped the flight bag and his arms circled tightly around her. His lips found hers and pressed them hungrily.

Her own heart seemed to have stopped, but she felt the beat of his against her chest, a beat strong enough to sustain both of them. She needed air, but it was painful even to think of turning her face from his. She tasted salt tears, tears of rapture. His? Her own?

And still they stood, totally wrapped in each other, until, at last, she gently pushed his face from hers. "Let me look at you." She traced his hollow cheek with her finger. "Are you really here?" She stood back, half expecting him to disappear even as she watched. "How?"

He took her in his arms again. "I'm really here, Ellen. As for how, we have our whole lives to talk about that."

He kissed her again, tenderly, on the lips, on her wet cheeks, on her upturned chin. "Oh, Ellen, what we've had to go through to find our way to each other."

They walked, at last, hand-in-hand, across the tarmac, drifting, without thinking, toward the little chapel. "Ron," she said softly, "I've changed. I thought I'd lost you forever, without ever having you." She longed to share her new life with Ron. Yet, she was having trouble finding the right words. "Losing you, I wanted you. But even more, I think, I wanted what you had."

He caressed her with his eyes, waiting for the words as if he expected them. "I found faith, Ron. I found him. I belong to Jesus now."

He nodded, tears in his eyes. "Ellen, I've been here for several days waiting for you to get back. So many people talked about how you had changed." Ron took her in his arms once more. She felt as if she had always lived within that protective circle. "I called my mother, too," he whispered, his lips brushing her ear.

Ellen winced.

"It's okay, darling. She would approve of anything I did right now." He smiled down at Ellen. "Besides, she read me your letter. Ellen, we're alive, both of us. And we're together, forever." Once more he held her in the back pew of the base chapel. And Ellen knew—they both knew—that God was not between them any longer. Now God held them both in the hollow of his loving hand.

Forever isn't very long, sometimes, on earth, in the middle of a war. "I haven't even reported in," Ellen said at last. "I have to, you know."

As they walked toward the hospital Ron began to answer the other questions. "The unimportant ones," he assured her.

"We heard there were only four chutes, Ron, and we knew it wasn't like you to bail out ahead of the crew. I guess that was the main reason I tried not to hope too much."

He shook his head sadly. "The back end of the plane took a bad hit, and we went totally out of control. We had a couple of Messerschmitts after us, so I told my co-pilot, engineer, and turret gunner to bail out. I went back to see what I could do."

She saw tears in his eyes. "I couldn't do much. Everything behind the bomb bay was already on fire. My bombardier was hit in the shoulder, and his chute was damaged. So I took hold of him, jumped, and we went down together."

"And made it," she gasped, "both of you? You were able to save him?"

"Actually, he saved me." Ron gripped her hand as he leaned on the cane. "The Germans only saw four chutes too."

He was silent for several minutes. "We hit hard. He landed on top of me. That's when . . ." he gestured to the stiffened right leg. "I couldn't walk. He could only use one arm, but he managed to bury the parachute and drag me under a hedge. Then he went off to find help. The Germans caught him and they found the chute. They found two of the other men dead, and the engineer alive, and they never looked for anybody else. When it got dark,

I crawled to a village and found a church. A French priest hid me."

"It was so long."

"Unfortunately, the village doctor was a collaborator, so the priest did the best he could with the leg. It didn't heal too well, but we expected American troops to arrive any day. We heard about the Normandy landings, of course, but for quite a while the Germans insisted that was a feint and expected another landing at Calais."

"Yes, the ruse worked well," she explained. "You know, we heard afterward that there were acres and acres of phony cardboard tanks, tents, all kinds of stuff planted all around Dover just to make them think that."

He touched her cheek. "They were ready for us at Calais, Ellen. If Ike had landed there it would have been a disaster. Anyhow, when we finally knew Calais had been by-passed, and when this darn leg got strong enough to sort of hold me up, I headed for our lines."

"Oh, Ron, if I had only known you were here! I took a vacation with Kim in Vermont."

"I tried to call you from London. The brass kept me there for a few days asking all kinds of questions about the fortifications around Calais and what I'd seen coming through the German lines. I wanted to see you, but I was afraid in a way. Ellen, I love you so much, but as far as I knew, you were still forbidden to me. And I felt so weak, much too weak, I confess, to resist the temptation."

His arm circled her waist and drew her closer. "I called Mom, and that's when she told me about your letter. Ellen, can you imagine how I felt when I heard those words?"

"Probably the same way I felt when I saw you on that runway."

She leaned against him, and he bent to kiss her forehead. "Something like that," he whispered.

Major Schaeffer proved to be tenderhearted under her stern military facade. Though Ellen had just returned from a leave, she found herself "temporarily unassigned." Ron was technically hospitalized and awaiting transport home. They spent three glorious days reliving old memories and exploring feelings they had never dared share before.

Ron had not asked her to marry him, so Ellen had not told him she would. *But I will*, she knew. *This war will be over in a few more months, and we'll be home, and we'll be together, totally, always.*

On Friday morning, Ron went shopping without her. "Somebody went and sent all my gear back to California," he explained with a grin. She hated letting him out of her sight, but, well, there was laundry to do, and she should write home.

That evening Ron took her back to the little town pub nearby, where the lights were dim and the jukebox was not too loud. "The food's still awful," she chuckled.

"The company's still good. Better than ever, in fact," he assured her.

"Ellen, my orders have come," he told her abruptly. "I sail from Southampton on Wednesday."

She stifled her gasp with her hand. "So soon?" she asked, knowing even as she spoke that the brief time they had had together was itself a miracle.

"We've been lucky to have this long, darling. They're sending me to Letterman for surgery. The doctors think they can take this knee apart there, and put it back together nearly as good as new. I was supposed to go a week ago, but I called in some favors."

"Letterman. San Francisco. So you'll be home in a couple of weeks, or nearly home anyhow. Ron, I'm so happy for you. And you know I'll be praying that the surgery goes well."

"I'll miss you." His voice cracked.

"I'll miss you." She swallowed the lump in her throat and tried to smile. "But it won't be long. The war is almost over."

"It will seem like an eternity. Ellen . . ." He fumbled in the pocket under his silver wings, the impressive row of battle ribbons and a new purple heart, and took out a tiny square box.

Shopping. She smiled, thinking of him hobbling the cobbled streets of this tiny English village looking for a ring. *As if we needed a ring to seal our love.*

"Ellen, there is a way you could go home with me, or at least right behind me."

He covered both her hands with one of his. "I love you so much. Ellen, will you marry me?"

"I thought you'd never ask," she whispered, leaning across the table to brush his lips with hers.

He slipped the simple diamond solitaire on her finger. It glistened in the light, and the tears of joy in her eyes turned the reflected light to tiny rainbows.

"Ron, I know, absolutely and without question, that God meant me for you. All I want is to go through the rest of my life with you, side by side. I love you." She studied once more the lines of his gaunt, beloved face. "I love you. All I want is to be your wife."

Planes roared overhead, violating their private moment. She tried to shut them out, but they kept coming. "As soon as this war is over, God willing, I will be your wife."

"Ellen, I mean now. I've checked. If we get married right away, here, you can apply for immediate discharge. You would be my wife before I left Southampton, and we could be together again in a matter of weeks."

Her first thought was to say yes. And so was her second thought, and her third. There was nothing on earth or in heaven that she wanted more at that moment. But she couldn't say it. "Ron, I want to. I want to so much. But I'm needed here for now. There are so many wounded and so few nurses. How can I think of my happiness, or even yours, precious as that is to me, when the need is so great? The war will be over soon, and then we will be together."

"We've waited so long, my darling." He gripped her hands. "Don't ask me to leave you again. Ellen, I want you." He stared at their clasped hands. "I need you."

"You know I want to be your wife, but how can I go home, now? How can I walk out on all those men in France?"

"If you love me . . ."

"I do," she vowed. "I do, but our love isn't the only thing on earth."

He didn't say anything, but his eyes pleaded with her.

"I could never forgive myself if I left before my job was done," she told him sadly.

"And I can't leave you here, in danger."

"Ron, if things were reversed, if I were going home and the choice was yours, would you feel the same way? Would you leave your men here to fight while you went home with your bride?"

"That's different," he protested. "Men fight wars to protect the women they love. I love you. I want you safe."

His hands squeezed hers, and she longed for his arms to hold her body as close. "I love you too much to let even my duty come between us, Ron," she said at last. "If you really want me to, I will marry you tomorrow and apply for my discharge."

He leaned across the table and kissed her tenderly. But the world would not be shut out. They both heard the incoming plane, sputtering, coughing, in trouble.

Ron sighed and kissed her once more. "If you took the easy way out you'd never forgive yourself, would you? One of the things I love about you is that stubborn idea you have that it's up to you to save the world."

"But I know now that I can't, Ron. What I want now is to make you happy."

"Love, honor, and obey?"

"Love, honor, and obey," she repeated softly. "Beautiful words, almost as beautiful as 'I love you.'"

He leaned back, then, and studied her intently. "You would do it for me, wouldn't you? But how would you feel later? Would you always wonder how many men died because you weren't there?"

"I don't know," she told him honestly.

"I don't know either, darling. I know what I want, but

219

I don't know what's right. Maybe this has to be your decision."

"No, not mine alone. Either way I know we will be married soon. We have to learn to make our decisions together, the two of us, with God. Ron, let's take our questions to him in prayer. If he wants me to go with you, I know I won't regret it."

They left the restaurant and drove back to the base in the little Austin that Ron had borrowed. At the door to the nurses' quarters they paused to pray together. Then they parted, reluctantly, but with a sure hope for the future.

She couldn't leave, she told him the next morning. Ron held her close, stroking her hair as he spoke. "I know. I hate it, but God showed me, too, that it wouldn't be right for us to put our own happiness ahead of the needs of so many."

Ellen felt the pain of being so close to him, and yet not one with him. "Ron, we can still be married right away," she told him. "We can be one, really one, even though we must be separated again for a little while."

She yielded to his embrace.

"It might only make the parting harder," he sighed, "but I'll gladly take that risk, if you will."

They filled out the necessary forms and got the necessary signatures. Somehow, as they remarked to each other, no one seemed very surprised.

Ellen took her turn scrounging the shops of the little English town. Although she couldn't find a wedding dress, she managed a little ivory pillbox hat and a yard of soft tulle to fashion a veil. She walked down the aisle of the base chapel in her crisp olive drab uniform, carrying the new ivory-bound Bible Ron had given her the night before. A phonograph cranked out the Wedding March.

The newlyweds spent their three-day honeymoon in a rainy Southampton, but the sun shone wherever they were. Even as Ellen stood on the dock waving to her husband as his ship sailed, she knew that he would have a safe voyage. And soon, very soon, they would be together again—together forever.

About the Author

Jean Grant was born in Michigan but has lived most of her life in northern California. She earned her bachelor's degree from the University of California at Berkeley, and has worked for more than thirty years as a clinical laboratory technologist.

Grant's first novel was The Revelation. Her articles and short stories have appeared in such publications as Evangelical Beacon, Mature Living, Home Life, Seek, and Power for Living. The Promise of Victory follows the first two books in the Salinas Valley Saga, The Promise of Peace and The Promise of the Willows.

The Salinas Valley Saga continues with
Book Four

The Promise of the Harvest

ð

Coming in Winter 1996